To my [...]
Happi Reading

Death by Numbers

Sam Harrison

Order this book online at www.trafford.com
or email orders@trafford.com

Most Trafford titles are also available at major online book retailers.

© Copyright 2012 Sam Harrison.

All rights reserved. No part of this publication may be reproduced, stored in a retrieval system, or transmitted, in any form or by any means, electronic, mechanical, photocopying, recording, or otherwise, without the written prior permission of the author.

Printed in the United States of America.

ISBN: 978-1-4669-4371-1 (sc)
ISBN: 978-1-4669-4370-4 (hc)
ISBN: 978-1-4669-4369-8 (e)

Library of Congress Control Number: 2012910963

Trafford rev. 07/12/2012

   www.trafford.com

North America & international
toll-free: 1 888 232 4444 (USA & Canada)
phone: 250 383 6864 ♦ fax: 812 355 4082

CONTENTS

Chapter 1. Trip to California 1
Chapter 2. The Game 7
Chapter 3. The Interruption 12
Chapter 4. Returning Home 21
Chapter 5. Monday Staff Meeting 29
Chapter 6. The Party 38
Chapter 7. Meeting with Suppliers 45
Chapter 8. Meeting with Bankers 53
Chapter 9. Suspicions 61
Chapter 10. Investigations Continue 71
Chapter 11. Pointed Questions 78
Chapter 12. More Bad News 87
Chapter 13. The Arrest 95
Chapter 14. It's Not Over 104
Chapter 15. A New Day 110
Chapter 16. New Evidence, New Arrest 118
Chapter 17. Interrogation Time 126
Chapter 18. Interrogating Paige 134
Chapter 19. The Search for Adam 142
Chapter 20. The Airport 151

CHAPTER 1

Trip to California

Mr. Ian Ianova, sole owner of Ianova Industries, left Toronto in his personal jet. En route to California, he reminisced about his successes during the twenty-eight years since he had taken over his Father's company.

Ian was going to sign up the largest deal for his company with his friend Tony Neil. Ian took along his sales manager, Peter Bixby. Peter normally signed the deals with the Neil Group with their head buyer, Carlos Ferrara, but this deal was so large that Ian and Tony Neil wanted to do it together, to see each other and talk about the old times. The Neil Group had been Ian's customer since the doors were opened. They supplied all the millwork products to condominium towers and hotel chains that the Neil Group developed and built. Tony Neil, the chief executive officer, had been—and still was—very happy with the product that Ian's company had provided over the years. They supplied kitchen cabinets, crown molding, baseboards, interior doorframes, and custom detailing for hotel lobbies and restaurants. As he had with many other customers, Ian had become very close friends with Tony.

After five hours in the air, Ian's Bombardier jet landed at LAX. Ian and Peter discussed some business as they waited for their golf clubs in the baggage area. Ian told Peter that he would handle the financial negotiations while Peter and Carlos discussed cabinet colors, trim colors, trim and cabinet styles, start dates, and frequency of deliveries. Ian and Tony were happy to let others handle the details.

Ian said, "Peter, with the exchange rate being so favorable, your pockets will be lined with money. Since this is a sixty-million-dollar deal, a 1 percent commission nets you a whopping $600,000, my friend!"

Peter replied, "You're going to give me the full point on this order?"

"Of course. Why wouldn't I? That's the contract we have together. You've done most of the work along with my estimating team. Besides, the company is doing great, and you deserve it!"

"Wow! Thanks, Mr. Ianova."

"Call me Ian—like you have for years. Why are you calling me Mr. Ianova?"

"Because you have no idea what this means to me."

"Whatever this means to you, Peter, I'm sure you will do whatever you need to in order to ensure your family is happy. After all, without a happy family, what else is there?"

Peter shrugged his shoulders and said, "You're right, Ian. Life is meaningless without a happy family."

Ian put his arm around Peter as they entered the limo to meet Tony and Carlos at the golf course. Ian tipped the busboys after they put the golf clubs in the trunk. Ian asked the driver to go directly to the Beverly Hills Country Club.

Peter asked, "Why are we going straight to the golf course instead of Tony's office?"

"The best deals in the world are made on the golf course, my friend. Where else and under what condition could you be with a top executive for five hours—and have them all to yourself?"

"But shouldn't we make the deal in the Neil Group's office first and then go golfing to celebrate?"

"Peter, the big deals are made on the golf course because it's the only place you can have peace of mind. Think clear. Know your objective. Know your budget—and where you need to be. Know how to get there. Know how to make your customer happy—even if you need to say what they need to hear. Most importantly, make the deal! That's called strategy, my boy. Besides, you'll have one of North America's largest land developers—who owns the company and happens to be a personal friend of mine—with you. Learn from him. He is an excellent businessman—as I am."

"Excellent logic," replied Peter. Peter had been a director of sales for more than twenty-five years, but hearing a successful company owner's fatherly advice felt special to Peter.

As they entered the driveway to the exclusive Beverly Hills Country Club, Ian looked over at Peter and said, "Remember to let Mr. Neil win. I can beat him because we are buds and will share wins over time, but it won't look good if you beat him too."

Peter smiled and said, "If I let Mr. Neil win—and you beat him—that means that I am letting you win too."

Ian smiled and got out of the limo. Peter chuckled and got out of the limo as well.

"Good to see you back, Mr. Ianova," said the concierge from the country club.

"Good to be back."

"Your usual is waiting for you before your one o'clock tee off, Mr. Ianova."

"Thanks so much," said Ian.

In the lounge area, Ian's Crown Royal and Coke awaited.

"I'll have the same," said Peter.

While Peter waited for his drink, Ian smiled and tasted his drink. He said, "Don't worry. Dana will be sure you are looked after."

Peter knew he'd better wait while Ian walked off to meet with Tony and Carlos. Tony got up when Ian turned the corner, and they made eye contact. Like college buds, they embraced in a bear hug along with back smacks. The usual jargon lasted until Peter arrived with his drink. Much to Carlos's delight, Tony noticed Peter and shook his hand.

Ian finally noticed Carlos and shook his hand. Tony looked at the fancy trim woodwork on the ceiling and said, "Carlos, that's why I always use Ianova Industries for all my projects. Look around you! It's beautiful. It's perfect—and it was supplied, delivered, and installed by my best friend, Ian Ianova."

"Thanks, Tony. I appreciate that." Ian hugged Tony again. Peter and Carlos looked at each other and sipped their drinks.

"Okay, boys. Are you all ready to swing the clubs?" Tony said.

Ian said, "Tony, tell me the truth. Did you warm up at the driving range before we arrived?"

Tony smiled. "What do you think? Did I?"

Ian said, "You're too smart as a businessman because you come prepared all the time. That's why you are so successful. I think you did go to the driving range first so that you are prepared."

Tony said, "If I beat you this afternoon, I did practice. If you beat me, I didn't practice."

Ian laughed and said, "That's good enough for me."

"Let's go then—and let the best team win," said Ian.

As they passed the pro shop on the way to their waiting golf carts, the club pro made eye contact with Ian and signaled him over.

Ian said, "See you at the tee box. I need to freshen up a bit."

He walked into the pro shop to see what Chris the pro wanted. "Tony had purchased the new 460cc King Cobra driver because he wanted to badly outdrive his buddy Ian." Ian laughed and thanked him for the info.

Ian said, "Why are you even telling me this?"

"Because the competition is good between you two, and you need to even the playing field a bit."

"How? I can't purchase the same driver. Tony will know something is up!"

Chris showed Ian the new Nike golf ball for women that he hadn't shown to Tony. The ball would travel at least fifteen yards farther on a drive than even the best of other golf balls.

"There is no insignia to indicate that it's a women's ball."

"Perfect! My ten-year-old small-head Calloway driver will do fine with this ball, and Tony won't know what hit him."

"Thanks, Chris. I'll take six balls."

After dropping a fifty-dollar tip, Ian walked towards the first tee box. The cart girl was starting her rounds and drove up to see if they need anything to drink or snack on. Ian grabbed a ride with the cart girl.

"The first round is on me," yelled Ian.

Tony yelled, "No, it's not. It's on me."

"Let's flip for it."

Tony yelled, "Tails!"

Rebecca grabbed a coin as she saw everyone struggling to find one. She offered to flip it.

Eager to see Rebecca move in any way at all, Tony, Ian, Peter, and Carlos yelled, "Yes!"

They looked at each other and laughed. Rebecca had no clue why they were laughing. When she laughed back, the boys laughed harder.

Rebecca flipped the coin, she tried to catch the coin in the air, but she missed, and the coin went into her top. There was a slight moment of silence as the men wondered who would grab the coin from her top. They all burst out in laughter, and Rebecca did too. The coin fell out and landed on tails.

Tony paid for the first round of drinks, and he was genuinely happy to do so.

CHAPTER 2

The Game

Tony grabbed a tee out of his bag and threw it into the air, when it landed on the ground, it pointed at Carlos. Carlos would tee off first. Tony threw the tee into the air again, and it pointed toward himself. Ian was next, and Peter would tee up last.

Carlos teed up and sent the golf ball about 240 yards down the fairway. It was hugging the right rough, but it was positioned well. Tony was proud of his new driver and took off the club cover; the distinct shine of a new club was present.

Ian said, "Oh, is that a new driver Tony?"

Tony said, "Yep, it sure is buddy. With this puppy, it's not a question of who will drive the ball farther; it's a question of how much farther will my drive be than yours?"

Ian laughed and said, "Those are fighting words."

Tony laughed as well. Tony teed up, and with a swift backswing and perfect downswing, he sent the ball into orbit at least 270 yards down the middle. Tony swirled the club like a pro to indicate how happy he was with the shot. Ian and the others indicated what a great drive it was. Ian teed up his ball and concentrated on his shot; he was motionless for five seconds. He addressed the ball and struck it at least 265 yards down the middle. It landed behind Tony's ball.

Tony said, "Great shot, Ian."

The others concurred. Carlos teed up and sent the ball 240 yards onto the fairway. Ian was extremely pleased with his shot. Peter and Ian got into their cart and started driving toward their golf balls.

Ian said, "My normal drive is about 255 yards, so I actually picked up ten yards by using the new ball recommended by the club pro."

Peter said, "Wow. I might go grab some of those balls after nine holes."

Ian smiled and said, "No, you're not!"

Tony and Ian made eye contact as they were driving their carts to their balls. Ian poked fun at Tony because his golf club in Toronto where he is a member has GPS in each golf cart.

Ian said, "Hey, where is the GPS?"

Tony smiled back at Ian and said, "I don't need GPS to know that I drove my ball farther than you did."

Ian and Tony laughed. Carlos and Peter put their second shots onto the putting green within twenty feet of the pin. Ian pulled out a wedge and placed the ball six feet from the cup. Tony pulled out a lob wedge and put the ball about twelve feet from the cup.

Ian smiled from cheek to cheek and said, "Tony, you hit your drive farther than mine, but it's all about the second shot, my friend."

Tony said, "I agree. In fact I'm so scared of my second shot that I hit my first shot as hard as I possibly could."

Everyone laughed. Carlos and Peter missed their putts but put them in next for par. Tony putted and missed but also got a par. Ian dropped his putt for a birdie. The fist pumping started, and everyone laughed.

"Call me Tiger, boys," said Ian.

The next eight holes were played with laughter and roasting. Rebecca came by again before they teed off at the tenth hole and promised not to throw anything down her top again. All four men were shaking their heads in disbelief at Rebecca's beauty and cuteness.

Carlos said, "Peter, I'd bring her home to meet my mom—even though I'm already married."

Peter laughed and said, "I've already dreamt that."

They both laughed. Ian bought rounds of drinks for everyone. Peter and Tony made eye contact again.

Ian said, "Tony, thank you very much for all the business you have given me over the decades."

"Are you kidding me?"

"No."

"Thank you!"

"It's not that often that you own a business you love, and have a customer such as yourself that I really care about. It makes work not seem like work. Not only are you a customer that I truly value, but you have ended up being one of my very best friends."

"You're getting too sentimental for me." Tony put his arm around Ian and guided him into the cart to carry on with the game.

As they were driving to the tenth tee box, Tony said, "You bid a hair over the $65 million mark on my next two projects. My budget was $60 million. I need you to be there. Can you do it?"

Ian paused to think. He turned to Peter and yelled, "Are there any custom colors on Tony's next projects or are they all standard products?"

Peter indicated that they are standard.

Ian looked at Tony and said, "I'll meet you halfway at $62.5 million." He stuck his hand out to shake Tony's hand.

Tony hesitated. That figure would put him over budget—and he would have to come up with the difference himself. "I love you buddy, but not enough to give you $2.5 million. I'll tell you what, let's do $61.5 million, and I'll get that money across the board by negotiating harder with the other trades." Tony stuck his hand out.

Ian wanted the job and knew Tony was over budget; he did not want to push Tony's bad button. He realized that he needed to make money for his company and was very confident that he would. He smiled, shook Tony's hand, and said, "Thanks for the work, Tony. It's a three-year project and will sure help keep all my employees busy."

Tony said, "It's all about the buck; isn't it, Ian? You're very welcome! And you have to promise me that you will come out here quarterly so we can play golf."

Ian said, "I wouldn't have it any other way."

Tony said, "I'll get my attorneys to draw up the contracts. Can your boys start with the preliminary work and design with my boys?"

"When can I get a copy of the contract?"

"In two weeks or less."

"Your word is gold to me, my dear friend."

Ian said, "It's a deal! Ian says to Peter, "I want you to go over the details and design with Carlos ASAP."

Carlos looked at Tony and nodded. Carlos had been with Tony for years. Tony knew what Carlos was thinking and returned the nod as if to say, "yes, proceed".

Ian said, "Tony, you have a wonderful relationship with Carlos."

Tony said, "And you do with Peter. It's important to have key people in your organization that you can trust because they are the people that make you the money."

Ian said, "People are like tools; you use tools to make your work easier. Without tools, you can't work."

Tony put his arm around Ian and said, "Great minds think alike. Let's play golf!"

Peter couldn't wait any longer. When the chance now comes as Tony and Ian drive away in their golf carts to start the next hole, Peter called his wife to tell her about the deal just made. Carlos is driving slowly so Peter can get the excitement out of his system. As soon she said hello, Peter says "We are rich!" Then he proceeds to tell her everything about the deal.

The rest of the game went off without a hitch. Everyone was happy with the outcome. Tony and Ian tied at 89. Ian could have had the game wrapped up, but he purposely missed the winning putt. Peter ended up with a 98 and Carlos had a 99, but neither was concerned about the outcome.

Tony went into the clubhouse while Ian washed his hands. Tony told Chris that the new driver had worked wonders. He dropped fifty bucks as a tip.

Tony went to wash his hands while Ian went into the pro shop. He said the new balls worked wonders and, his accuracy and added distance made Tony take notice. He dropped an additional fifty dollar tip.

Chris said, "Thanks. If I can help you further in any way, please let me know."

Ian thanked him again and walked away.

Chris walked back behind the counter. *Who is the businessman now, dudes? Oh yeah!*

CHAPTER 3

The Interruption

As Peter and Ian boarded the plane back to Toronto, Ian took a call from Ron William Branson of R. W. Branson. Their friendship had lasted as long as their working relationship—at least twenty years. Ron was CEO of a national hotel chain that used Ian's company to supply and install all the cabinets and millwork products.

"Ian speaking."

"Hello. How are you, Ian?"

"I'm fine. How are you?"

"I could be better."

"What is the problem?"

"Your trim products in the hallways of my new hotel in Palm Springs are not consistent with each other and appear to be different colors. I cannot accept this, Ian. I have a grand opening in two weeks, and the product looks like crap. I need you to fix it."

"I'll tell you what. I am at LAX en route to Toronto. I will tell my pilot to stop in Palm Springs first. Can you meet me on site, Ron? We'll address the problem."

"Absolutely," said Ron.

Ian called up to his pilot and told him to set a new flight plan for Palm Springs.

The pilot said, "Okay, Mr. Inaova, rerouting to Palm Springs. The new flight plan will take five or ten minutes, and then we'll taxi out."

Ian took a call from his company financial controller, Ben Clipfeld.

"What's up, Ben?"

"Have you seen the foreign exchange rate, Ian?"

"I haven't seen it today, but I know it's around 45 percent in our favor."

"Guess again."

"Listen to me, Ben—and listen closely. I own the company—not you. I ask the questions, and you answer them. I'm guessing nothing. What are you trying to tell me? Say what you need to say since it's you that phoned me. I've got a lot on my mind."

"Sorry, Ian. The exchange rate was sitting at 30 percent, and the consensus was that this trend will continue."

"You mean our Canadian dollar is getting stronger?"

"Yes, it is. It's been happening for about five months. What are you doing to cut costs?"

"Nothing," said Ben. "I'm waiting on direction from you, Ian."

"Are you crazy, Ben? Why in God's name are you waiting on direction from me? Aren't you the controller? Control the company, damn it! How can we have a fifteen-point swing like that and you do nothing about it? That kind of swing comes right off the bottom line. We contract some jobs with loss margins sometimes because we are competitive solely because of the dollar exchange and make it up that way. With a swing of fifteen points, we are losing money, Ben!"

Ben was afraid to say anything.

"Ben, are you there?"

"Yes, sir. I am." Ben sounded as if he had been spanked. "I'm sorry, Ben."

"Things are good and then bad. I signed the biggest deal this company has ever seen with the Neil Group. Now I wonder if it is such a great deal with this exchange rate news you gave me Ben." And just before I took your call, Ron of R.W. Branson called to say he was not happy with our product in Palm Springs. I wonder how deep that problem will be."

"Wow. Sorry, Ian. I should have been more sensitive."

"No, it's okay. You didn't know. Besides, none of us has crystal balls. We can't tell the future, and things happen. One way or another, we will make this work out. Call in our bankers and see if we can hedge some funds. Check to see if we can hold onto collections longer and deposit a greater amount if they will give us a better rate. One thing is for sure—see if we can double up some jobs in the plant and let some people go. Call in our top suppliers and tell them I want an emergency meeting this Monday in my office. We need sixty- to ninety-day terms."

"Consider the meeting done, but we already are on sixty- to ninety-day terms. In fact, the suppliers are demanding a meeting with you."

Ian looked as if he had swallowed a tennis ball and he couldn't breathe. He had a look of panic. "See you when I get back."

"Okay, Ian. Have a great flight."

"Thanks. Before you hang up, put me through to my son. Okay?"

"Hi, Dad," said Robert.

"Hello, son. What are you up to?"

"Oh not much, Dad, usual stuff. You know, doing all your work here, looking through *Auto Trader* online, hoping you'll buy me a Corvette or a Viper, and getting ready to pick our weekly lottery numbers for this week's draw."

"Well, son, you'd better pray for those lottery numbers to come in because you'll never get a Corvette or a Viper from me when you're only seventeen years old."

"Come on, Dad. A lot of rich kids' parents buy them cars."

"I agree. I will as well, but it will be a Honda Accord or a Ford Focus—something more practical."

"Dad, I guess I'll take your advice and start praying for the lottery numbers to come in because I don't like those old man cars that you like. The only problem is there are twenty-five of us here who pool our money for the lottery. Even if we win, my share of the winnings probably won't be enough to buy toothpaste."

"Ha! Think big, son. You never know—you all could win the big one."

"Only in La La Land, Dad."

"How much is the big one incidentally?" asked Ian.

"This one is huge because there was no winner on the last two draws; the grand prize has been carried over. This draw is about $275 million."

"Wow. That would be sweet to win, Robert. That would help pay for the ski trip you and your buddies are taking in December."

"Sure will, Dad."

"Do me a favor, son. Buy me ten tickets and leave them in my top drawer in my office."

"Wow, my dad is a gambler. Cool, sure, Dad, I'll get them for you."

"Pull out the work orders for Branson Hotels in Palm Springs and let me know what color the project has chosen for its stain."

"Okay, Dad. Give me a second here. I'll pull it up on my computer screen. It's the cognac color."

"Oh no. That color varies too much, and I think Ron Branson has a keen eye for it. He will not accept variations."

"Come on, Dad. You know wood accepts stain differently."

"Of course I know that. I think Ron knows that as well. I have a feeling it's not that simple. Ron wouldn't call me if it was a matter of wood taking stain differently. The problem, I'm sure, stems deeper than that."

"You're probably right, Dad. What are you going to do?"

"I am going to fly there and check it out this afternoon, son."

"I thought you would be home tonight, Dad."

"Things change, son."

"We'll see you tomorrow?"

"No. I'll still see you tonight—much later tonight, that's all."

"Mom wanted to talk to you. She is right here."

"Hello, darling," said Leah. "What am I overhearing from Robert? Are you going to be late tonight?"

"I will be late. I must go to Palm Springs to see Ron. There is a problem with our product that I need to review with him."

Leah tangled the phone line with her fingers, wearing a devilish smile. "Are you sure you are going to be late?"

"Yes. I am, sweetie."

"Should I wait up for you?"

"Mom!" shouted Robert.

"Ha!" said Ian. "You are sounding too sexy for Robert, but I love it when you talk like that to me. No, don't wait up for me. I'll be quiet when I arrive. Love you."

"Love you, too."

Peter was staring out the window at one of the runways as they taxied for takeoff. It was driving him nuts—especially after overhearing the exchange rate fiasco. Peter was wondering what that was all about.

"Oh my God," said Peter. "That didn't sound like a positive phone conversation. How bad do you think the exchange rate will hurt us?"

"It'll hurt real bad, Peter." Thinking about the huge commission that might be erased, Peter couldn't help but think of the phone call to his wife.

Peter said, "I can take a .5 percent commission drop on the Neil Group deal if that will help you out."

Ian looked at Peter in disbelief and said, "That is an excellent gesture, and I really, really appreciate that. However, I think our problems are going to be much deeper than a point or half a point here or there. If the exchange rates keep changing, our profits will be wiped out faster than you can finish a meal. Remember, our business was at least 80 percent shipments to the U.S. We need to trim the fat in our company. People have been living high for too long. Company cars, gas cards, insurance, great benefit packages—I need to fix all that."

Ian was perplexed by the generous offer from Peter. He said, "Thanks, but we'll get through this one way or another."

Peter and Ian look out the window over Palm Springs and landed a few moments later. Neither said a word while they got the rental car and started driving toward Ron Branson's office.

While in the car, Ian looked over at Peter and said, "This is not good. I have a bad feeling about this."

Peter was reluctant to respond, thinking whatever he would say would be incorrect. They pulled into Ron's parking lot and made their way up to the reception area.

"Good afternoon, Mr. Ianova," said the receptionist.

"Good afternoon," replied Ian. "I am here to see Ron."

"He is expecting you, Mr. Ianova. Please sit down, and I will let him know you are here. Water or coffee for either of you?"

"No thank you."

"Mr. Branson, Mr. Ianova is here to see you."

"Send him in," replied Mr. Branson.

"Mr. Ianova, follow the hallway down to the—"

Ian said, "I know where it is. Thank you."

"Welcome back to Palm Springs, Ian."

"Great to be back," replied Ian. "You remember Peter, my sales manager?"

"Of course I do," replied Ron. "This is Tia, my assistant."

"Yes, I remember her. I wish I was coming here for golf."

"Yes, I wish so too," replied Ron. "It's best we go to site so that you can see firsthand what the problem is. I totally understand the characteristics of wood and how it takes stain and the tolerable variances and so on. This is not that issue. I've completed several hotels with your firm and understand what is right and what is not right. I'm afraid this is not right. Let's go to site now. Do you all want to come with me and then I will take us all out to dinner?"

Ian smiled. "No thanks, Ron. I appreciate your offer, but this was a surprise trip. We are unfortunately committed early tomorrow morning, so I would rather take our rental vehicle and follow you so we can go directly to the airport once we are done on-site."

"Okay Ian, but it has been almost a year. You need to make time to come out here for golf during your winter."

"That is a date, I truly look forward to that considering the winters we have" replied Ian.

Ian drove with Peter. "There is not even a chance I could have brought out the variances in a natural product like wood. Ron sure is knowledgeable and knows his stuff."

"He sure does," replied Peter. "That is what scares the crap out of me. I believe the entire site is screwed; otherwise our service department would have cleaned it up."

"You're right," said Peter.

At the job site, they were greeted by the site super. His name was Bob.

The hotel lobby was luxurious.

"This is incredible," said Ian.

"Wow this is gorgeous," said Peter.

"Yes, it turned out lovely," said Ron.

Near the hotel lobby bar, Ian noticed a massive variation in the stain color on the trim around the bar. He clearly could see what Ron was talking about.

As they got to the bar, Ron said, "You see this work? This finish, I'm sorry, it was not acceptable to me. It needs to be redone. Sure it looks great from a distance as you walk in and look around however, when you get close, it's just not right. I will wait here. Please go walk the hallways with Peter and converse with each other. Walk a few floors; you will see that this problem exists throughout the building."

Bob said, "The interior kitchenettes are all okay for some reason. They all match. It's the trim, the crown molding, the floor baseboards, and the lobby trim."

Ian and Peter started looking around. The trims were terrible. Ian could not understand the variance in the trims when the kitchens were all okay. He had seen enough after walking five floors with Peter. They made their way back to the lobby to meet Ron and Bob.

"What do you think?" asked Ron.

Ian said, "I need to go back to my office to speak to my people so we can come up with a cure."

Ron said, "This needs to take priority when you get back to your office. The grand opening is only four weeks away. If there is a delay, the interest costs I incur will sink your company, I will not absorb them, and I will not open this hotel with that product. So go back and please speak to your people, but do it fast and fix this quick."

"Leave it with me," replied Ian with an unsure look in his eye. "I will look after you."

They all shook hands and parted company. Ian and Peter got back into their rental car and made their way back to the airport.

Ron said, "Tia, write everything down that transpired today in detail, date it, e-mail Ian and Peter the minutes, and file it. You never know if we'll need it if we go to court. I have a feeling we may."

"Consider it done, Mr. Branson."

Not a word is said between Ian and Peter on their way back to the airport. Ian is so upset at the quality that he has just seen, it is sickening. They go through the motions of returning the rental car and signing off the visa slip and make their way towards the gate for private aircraft departures.

CHAPTER 4

Returning Home

As they are boarding the plane, Ian looked at Peter and said, "There are seventy floors. My cost is probably $150,000 per floor. You do the math; this will cost me millions. And I have to pay to remove the old stuff too. What went wrong here? Peter, do you know? If you do and you didn't tell me."

"I knew nothing. If I heard anything, I would have said something immediately."

"I sure hope so. I'm pissed off. There is no need for what I saw."

Peter kept quiet because Ian was as upset as he had ever seen him.

As they make their way to their seats on the aircraft, Ian checked his cell phone and read a text from the company controller. The Canadian dollar had gained more strength. Ian was visibly upset as most of his business was in the United States. With all that was going on, his face was turning white. Peter was very quiet; Ian was steaming. Ian dialed the office with his cell and got reception to page his plant manager.

"This is Joe speaking, how can I help you?"

"Hi, Joe, how are you, this is Ian?"

"I am ok, how are you Ian?

"I've had better days, and this business trip I'm on sucks. All I am hearing is bad news and dollars being tossed out into the wind."

"What is happening?"

"All the trim did not match at the Branson job, Joe. They were different colors."

"How about the wood? Is it a consistent grain?"

"Joe, it's not the wood. The stain had too much pigment in some cases; in other cases it's sporadic like there was too much air pressure in the spray guns. In some cases, it's too blotchy. The quality was not there and Ron wanted all this stuff replaced. Quite frankly, I can't blame him. It looked like shit! This was your responsibility, Joe. You get paid to make sure this doesn't happen. I have a meeting with the suppliers and bankers this coming Monday afternoon that Ben arranged. Get the assistant plant manager and the sprayers ready for a meeting Monday morning. I want answers as to what went wrong and what the cure is. We are in deep shit here. Between the dollar problem and this problem, it might sink the company. We better think of a way to solve this stain issue fast and cheap." Ian slammed the phone and hung up.

Peter was afraid to even breathe too loud at this point.

Ian asked, "Do you have any opinion as to what the problem is here?"

Peter replied, "I noticed some hairline cracks on the curves of the crown molding. That means that veneer material was used. If veneer was used, there are two problems. First, we were contracted to use solid wood because that's what Ron wanted because it's a high-end project. Secondly, because the veneer was as thin as paper, the stain didn't sink in enough to give it a rich, deep lustrous color. If

Ron ever finds out veneer was used, he will hit the roof because he undoubtedly will feel that we cheated him."

Ian said, "That's why the kitchens all look great; it's all solid wood. I noticed that when I looked at the grain around the arch tops of the cabinet doors. I noticed the grain cuts at the top that you only get when solid wood is used."

"That's right," said Peter. "Somehow we cheated Ron."

"Damn it. I never gave instructions to our plant people to cheat on any order any time. That is not the way that Ianova Industries does business. My reputation is based on quality workmanship and on-time delivery with competitive rates. Besides, no one in the plant would send veneer on a project—especially when we write the production specs. It went through the order process so there shouldn't be any confusion there. I'll tell you, Peter, if I hear of anyone at Ianova Industries doing something that wasn't right, I will fire them. You wrote the spec, Peter; any chance you were wrong?"

"No way," said Peter. "No way at all."

"Yeah, I believe that."

The radio control tower radioed the pilot of Ian's jet and indicated to head toward runway four and await landing of a heavy passenger jet prior to takeoff. Ian's pilot repeated the instructions and subsequently followed the instructions. Ian's jet taxied toward the runway and stopped.

Ian noticed the plane stopped and radioed up to the pilot to ask what was going on. The pilot explained that they were waiting for a large passenger aircraft to land on their runway first.

"How long do we have to wait asks Ian? I see the jet in my sites sir. Probably another minute or so because I see him touching ground now so we can roll shortly Mr. Ianova. Ok says Ian. It will be a smooth flight Mr. Ianova you can enjoy some nice sleep time, sir."

"Sounds great. Will the nice sleep time cost me any money?"

"Excuse me, sir? I do not understand your question."

"It's all right. Don't worry about it. Let's say it's been a tough couple days, and nothing has been free."

"I see sir, sorry to hear about that. (in the back ground you can hear the control tower saying that Ian's jet is ready to take off at will) I heard that, I'll leave you alone to fly this plane. Thank you sir, I will have you airborne in no time so you can relax. Enjoy the flight, Mr. Ianova."

"Thanks. I will," said Ian.

As the plane ascends, a great view over Palm Springs has taken Ian aback. Ian looked over at one the famous casinos.

"Peter, there is a lot of history at that casino down there. I'm not even sure of the name since it has been bought and sold so many times over the years. At one time it was called Shore's Dollars; maybe it was named after Dina Shore. There are a lot of stories inside those walls. One comes to mind. It's about a great buddy of mine who died in a head on collision with another driver, his name was Bill Henderson. He was my partner here at Ianova Industries. He was the son of my dad's partner. Mr. Henderson and my dad started Ianova Industries. Actually, my dad started the company, and Mr. Henderson bought into it because my dad needed money—and Mr. Henderson had money. Anyways, Bill was Mr. Henderson's son. I ended up being very good friends with Billy boy. But Billy had a bit of a problem as we were growing up. He loved fishing, women, and gambling, and sometimes, not in that order,. He would give up a good lay if he could get time in a casino. He loved gambling. We were in Palm Springs for business together once, and Billy insisted we go to the casino before flying back home. We didn't have our own plane then, so we couldn't ask the pilot to delay takeoff like we can now. So we spent an hour at the casino. When it was time to leave, Billy had to make one more bet. We were in such a rush; we had about one hour to be on the plane and we were still in the casino. San Francisco had won the Super Bowl and the casino was taking bets on the next year's winner. Billy slapped a thousand bucks on a team with high odds because it was a low favorite. We just made it back to the airport in time to catch our flight by seconds. Anyways, a year went by and what happens? Bill's team came in and won. I can't even remember who the team was—so don't ask. The winnings paid $750,000. Not bad. We were so busy at work, trying to grow the company. As we were getting busier and busier, it took Bill almost one year to go back and claim his winnings. The casino had a rule that the winner had to come back to claim the winnings; they wouldn't mail a check or anything like that. He flew down here and picked up his check. I never saw him again."

"What happened?" asked Peter.

"Bill died. He was a victim of his own life. He went to the casino, gambled, went to a bar, got drunk, picked up a woman, had fun with her, got back in his car, crossed the solid line, and had a head-on collision with a truck. The truck won, and Bill lost. Wish he was still here. Even with his vices, he was a smart businessman—and we were making money, a lot of money."

"Sounds like you miss him, Ian."

"It's not too often you have a business partner who also is a friend. Sure wish I could win money like Billy did. By the way, have you heard how much this week's lottery is? It's over $275 million. That would be one hell of a winning, wouldn't you say?"

"Absolutely, Ian."

"Did you buy tickets?"

"I did," said Peter.

"All my business woes would be over if I won that. How many tickets did you buy, Peter?"

"I bought fifty of them. Wow, good for you. It's only good if I win; other than that, it's money down the drain."

"What will you do if you win?"

"A new Ferrari, a new house, and a vacation property."

"That sounds like a great dream, I hope you get to realize it. Get some sleep now Peter"

"I will try to Ian"

"I'm going to try to get some shuteye but I must read these financials first."

Ian called Robert. "Do me a favor, son, go get me $500 worth of tickets for this week's lottery." Ian kept his voice low so Peter would not hear him.

"Are you kidding? I already bought you ten like you asked and put them in your top drawer."

"We need to win."

"Dad, the chances aren't good; you know that."

"What's going on?"

"Robert, it's complicated. Things aren't going the way they should."

"Okay, Dad. I'll do it."

"Who was on the phone, Robert?" asked Leah.

"Dad asked me to buy ten lottery tickets for him the last time we spoke, and he called me to ask me to get him another five hundred tickets and that things were not going well. What's up with that?"

"Your dad wants tickets because he wants to win. I want to win too. I want to join your pool at work. How can I do that?"

"Give me five bucks, and I will tell Paige to add your name to the pool. You will be the twenty-fifth person."

"Great. I hope we win."

Ian looked over his financial statements that Ben had emailed him and saw that his company was making money at the 45 percent exchange rate he thought he was getting. He got his calculator and deducted 15 percent. He saw that his company was losing money. He was very upset with Ben since this swing had taken place over a few months—with Ben saying nothing. The suppliers were upset as they were on long payment terms. He thought he could talk the suppliers into longer terms, but Ben had done that already. Ian put his head down and shook it in disgust.

"Thank Goodness it's Friday. I can relax this weekend and think of what to say on Monday for the bankers and to our suppliers. God help me."

As Peter and Ian land in Toronto Peter wakes up and asks Ian how he slept. Ian looks at Peter and says

"I didn't sleep. I tried but couldn't. But you on the other hand Peter, wow, can you ever snore."

"Oh no, sorry Ian that's why you probably couldn't sleep, my snoring kept you awake." "No that's not why Peter, I have too much on my mind."

Both walked out and headed into separate limos for the ride home.

"Good evening sir," said the limo driver.

"Good evening, Rex."

"How was the lovely West Coast on this trip, sir?"

"The beauty is always refreshing, but the meetings were something I would not wish on any enemy."

"Sorry to hear that, Mr. Ianova."

"Well, whatever the future holds, we'll get through it one way or another."

"Yes, sir. I agree—no mountain big enough."

Ian got out of the limo in front of his house and was greeted inside his front door by Leah and Robert. They both decided to stay up late and wait for Ian to come home.

Robert gave his dad the lottery tickets and reminded him that the other ten were in his top drawer.

Ian said, "Thanks son."

"You're welcome, Dad."

Robert walked away and Leah hugged Ian.

"What's happening, Ian? This is not like you to scurry around to buy lottery tickets for Goodness sakes. We don't need the money. I want to know what is going on."

"Come with me, honey. Help me get settled in. Let's have a glass of wine, and I'll fill you in."

"Okay, but make it fast. It's eleven thirty, and we need to get to bed."

Leah kissed Ian. "Okay, let's go,"

CHAPTER 5

Monday Staff Meeting

"Good morning, Mr. Ianova," said Vanity Leyland.
"Good morning, Vanity."
"Coffee, sir?"
"Yes, the usual. Get Ben in my office."
"Okay, sir."
As Ian walked into his office, he saw his Mom vacuuming.
"Mom, what are you doing?"
"I'm vacuuming. What does it look like I'm doing?"
Barbara was a warm old lady. She was sweet and caring and always smiling. She was so approachable that the office staff confided in her often regarding their own personal tribulations.
Vanity walked into Ian's office with his coffee and said, "Good morning, Mrs. Ianova. I didn't know you were here. What can I get for you?"
Barbara grabbed Ian's coffee from Vanity's hands and said, "Nothing, dear. Thank you so much for asking." She grabbed a

coaster and placed Ian's coffee on the coaster. "You think you are so grown up, but you'll always be my baby."

"I guess you'll never let me change that."

"No, son. I won't."

Barbara began to put the vacuum away as Ben walked into Ian's office.

"What the heck have you done with my company?"

Barbara came out of Ian's closet after putting the vacuum away and said, "Ian Ianova, don't address anyone in that manner! Your father and I started this company by treating people as equals to us. Don't be so rude!"

"What the heck is going on, Ben?" asks Ian again totally ignoring his Mother.

"Things got out of hand real fast, and I tried to handle things the way I thought was right without consulting you. It got worse, Ian. On Friday, the Canadian dollar gained another two points; that's a 17 percent gain in a few months. It was killing us. Our operating line of credit was maxed at $15 million and the bankers want answers. Our suppliers were at sixty- to ninety-day terms already, and some had put us on COD. We're in trouble, Ian."

"All you have done is play with the money," said Ian. "You haven't made us money, Ben."

"What do you mean, Ian? How can I make you money when we are losing money?"

"I expect you to bring in suppliers, ask for special discounts because of the exchange issue—of which we had no control over—and get it from them. I expect you to bring in our plant managers and double up some positions and let some people go. I don't expect you to incur more debt by increasing our operating line so we pay higher interest on something at this point we can't afford. I expect you to have a plan like you're paid to do. I expect you to do your job!"

The office staff could hear Ian yelling at Ben; they had never heard Ian yell before. Ian unloaded on Ben.

Barbara walked into Ian's office and said, "What has gotten into you, Ian? The whole staff is upset."

"Mom, not now. I've got meetings with the plant managers and bankers, and I need to get on top of what is happening."

"What is happening, son?"

"Mom, please not now. I will fill you in. I promise you. Ben, get the plant managers in here and Paul Lazarus."

"Don't make it a long time from now, Ian," said Barbara. "I want to know what is happening."

"Okay, Mom, I promise to fill you in."

Joe, Albert, and some stain sprayers walked into Ian's office along with Ben. Joe was Ian's right-hand man when it came to production.

"Good morning to all," said Ian. "What went wrong with the product at Branson's project?"

Joe said, "Ian, after investigating, it looked like a few things went wrong. First the sprayer we used on Branson's job had the mixer inside the canister seized when spraying. Blotchiness was the result."

"You mean the agitator got seized?"

"Yes, that is what I mean."

"Yeah but the pigments will all get stuck to the bottom of the canister if the agitator is seized when spraying. How did we get color?"

"The sprayer would simply shake the canister before each spray with his hands."

Ian put his head down in disbelief and shook his head while rubbing his forehead.

"Why didn't we change spray canisters with one of the fifty high-tech modern ones we have that work?"

"The sprayer was too lazy to change canisters because the color was already poured, and it was a chore to clean the canister and get a new one."

"But the blotchiness was consistent throughout the project. It took months to complete. How do you explain the consistent inconsistency?"

"The sprayer never changed canisters. The same broken canister was used."

"Who was the sprayer?"

"It was Jose."

Ian looked at Jose and said, "What do you have to say for yourself?"

Jose said, "I thought I was doing the right thing by being fast."

"You thought you were doing the right thing by being fast? You're an idiot! You're fired; get out of my sight."

"You can't fire me. I have a family and a mortgage, sir. I need the money."

"You have no idea what you have done here. You cost my company millions of dollars, and you could cause a lot more people to lose their jobs here because of your stupid actions. Get out."

Jose didn't move.

Ian looked to Ben and said, "Get him out of here."

Ben looked at Jose and said, "Come on. Let's go."

Ben and Jose left.

"Joe, I can't believe you weren't on top of this. Albert, I can't believe you were not on top of this either."

Ben walked back in.

Joe said, "There was also another issue. We used veneer wood instead of solid wood on the trim work. I let it ride even though I had clear knowledge of the spec."

"Why?" said Ian.

"We were out of material and had to wait a month for solid or two days for veneer. I opted for veneer as it was half price. Imagine if it all worked out how far ahead we would be."

"Damn it, Joe. That's not what this company is all about; we were not to cheat our customers. Since day one, we have prided ourselves on quality, on-time delivery, top-notch installation, and industry-leading after-sales service. You have put this company on the verge of bankruptcy. I have millions of dollars of errors to fix at Branson's job. That's the cost if all goes well. Where will this money come from, Joe?"

"I don't know," said Joe.

"How far ahead are we on production right now?" asked Ian.

"Also, while we are talking, Ian, our work order department had made a design error on handicap code production on all of our Los Angeles projects."

"Where's Paul? He's work order, right? I asked you to bring him in here."

"He stepped out," said Ben.

"Call my son in here."

"Apparently, they drew production for another state's specifications without changing specs when starting to draw the California projects."

"You have got to be frigging kidding me!"

Robert and Ben walked into Ian's office.

"Robert, what the hell happened in LA?"

"Dad, the fellow drawing the Florida projects also draws the California projects. He finished drawing a project in Florida that we have. He then started to draw a California project. His spec book was still open to Florida handicap codes. The codes between Florida and California were different."

"How can they be different? Isn't the code federal?"

"No. Each state can decide handicap codes. That was the problem in this case. Therefore, while drawing California, he drew Florida specs, and they were wrong."

"How many projects are we talking about here?"

"All of them," said Robert.

Ian asks again, "How many projects are we talking about?"

"Eight," said Robert.

"My Goodness. What's the cost to repair this problem? Anyone figure this out?"

"One million per project is what we estimate," said Ben.

"Eight million dollars? I can't believe this. Where is Paul Lazarus? The friggin' guy is in charge of our work order department, and he is not even here when he created this friggin' mess in the first place..."

Paul Lazarus walked into the room with a massive smile on his face.

Ian said, "Paul, under your watch, it seems you have let slip through your fingers the largest error this company has ever made."

"Well, sir," said Paul. "It's like this, fire me—I really don't care because my share of the $275 million grand prize is $11 million. So fire me."

"Are you serious?"

"I sure am," said Paul.

Robert smiled from cheek to cheek. "We won the big prize!"

Barbara walked in with a serious look and went straight to Ian. She slapped him across the face and yelled, "I've overheard enough. You've put incompetent people in position to watch over a company that your father started with his own two hands. These people you put into position. It's your problem—not theirs. What have you done to this company? Ben, you are as useless as a three dollar bill. You're no controller; you even lied about your bachelor's degree. That's right, I checked. My bright son didn't. Joe, if you cared at all about this company instead of constantly looking at your watch because five o'clock couldn't come fast enough, you would had caught the canister issue. You should have ordered solid product in time to meet delivery deadlines; instead you let things ride because you are incapable of smart decisions and have no thought process to look ahead to see what specifications were forthcoming—like the incapable decision my son made when he hired a useless piece of trash like yourself who finds time to surf porn rather than do his job. Paul, I am most disappointed in you. You were in debt, about to lose your family and your home, because of your gambling addiction. My son put you through therapy, and you got your family and your home back. This company treated you like a son. This company matched your maximum annual savings contribution to make a better man out of you—so you can provide a retirement for them and yourself—and this is the thanks we get? That's the best you have because your share of the winnings is $11 million, then you say fire me!,—and we all are a piece of shit now? I wipe my ass with your money. My fortune is well over ten times your fortune. I will spend a tenth of my money to prove you sabotaged this company with your poor decisions. I'll make sure you spend all your winnings in legal fees defending yourself. You did not live up to your fiduciary responsibility. Should I do that to you? Don't forget, Paul, that this company made you a man. Get out of my face. Ben, Paul, Joe, get lost. You're all fired."

Ben said, "You can't fire me without severance. I know the laws."

Barbara walked over right to Ben and said, "Then sue me. You know where to find me. I'll be rebuilding this company that you helped knock down. Paul, Joe, you also sue me, but get out of my face—all of you. Ian, if you weren't my son, you'd be fired too."

Paul, Joe, and Ben walked out.

"Ian, shame on you—golfing, drinking, and good times allowed you to let your guard down. You put this company on the verge of bankruptcy and it looks like Chapter 11 may be the only solution to get out of this mess. I will bring in my own bookkeeper and my own company lawyer. Dune, come in here. Gentlemen, meet Dune Marsland. He is the new controller. I smelled trouble here. I brought Dune in last month. He has been working nights so no one would know he was here. He gave me a report this morning. It's disgusting. He knew more about the trouble we were in than you did, Ian. Albert, you know what you were doing. I read your reports. I saw that you were aware of the atrocities going on and didn't say anything because of your loyalty to Joe. Be loyal to me, Dune, and Ian now. I trust you—and Ian will trust you. You are the new plant manager. Make things happen back there."

"Thank you, Mrs. Ianova," said Albert as he walked out. "I won't let you down."

"Grandma, you and my dad can have my $11 million to turn this company around."

"Thank you, Robert. That is sweet. That's why Grandma loves you; you have my generous qualities. Keep it for now. Go join your peers and enjoy the party of winners."

"Okay, Grandma. I love you."

"I love you, too."

"See you, Dad."

"See you, son."

Barbara turned to Ian and said, "Tony Ianova—the love of my life, my husband for fifty years, your father, the founder of Ianova Industries—would roll over in his grave if he knew what position this company is in. In your meetings, I'll be listening."

When Barbara walked out, Ian said, "God help us, Dune."

CHAPTER 6

The Party

Robert walked into the work order department. The celebrations were running wild. Everyone was mentioning that they won $275 million instead of the split of $11 million because it sounded so much nicer. Party streamers were flowing through the air; everyone was in such a joyous mind-set. Happy screams were everywhere.

Paul was in the office and broke the news that he was fired. He didn't care because of his winnings.

Robert overheard him and got very upset. He said, "Did you hear nothing my grandmother said to you? Have you no respect at all for what this company did for you? Hey, we all made mistakes."

"Robert, back off," said Paul.

"I know we all made mistakes," said Robert. "But you were mocking us. That was a piss-poor attitude—and I don't like it."

"What are you going to do about it, kid?" said Paul.

Robert said nothing.

"I don't want to injure my pretty fist by hitting your ugly face, old man."

Paul pushed Robert. That's all Robert needed to wind up and punch Paul right in the face. Paul went flying back and ended up flat on a table full of deserts. Everyone started freaking out a bit.

Paige Plane yelled, "Hit him again—he deserves it. He was an ass."

Paul got up and took a swing at Robert. Robert ducked and nailed Paul in the stomach and face.

Robert said, "Have you had enough, old man? I told you I didn't want to injure my pretty fist from hitting your ugly face—and now my pretty fist is bleeding."

Robert bent down over Paul and wiped his bleeding fist on Paul's white shirt. All of a sudden, whack, a kick to the side of Paul's stomach came out of nowhere. Robert was stunned by where it came from. Paige had kicked Paul.

Robert said, "Stop it, Paige. What are you doing?"

"I hate him," said Paige.

"Okay. I can see that, but leave him alone."

People dispersed as Paul got up. His wits were coming back slowly.

Robert said, "You're not welcome here. You'd better leave."

Paul said, "I don't want to be here. I'm leaving. I carpooled here with Chris, John, and Phil. I need to gather them so we can all leave."

"You go wait outside," said Robert. "I'll get them for you."

Chris, John and Phil had seen what happened and knew why Robert was approaching them.

Chris said, "I guess we are all leaving since we came with Paul."

Robert smiled and said, "Hey, with all your money, stay behind and take a limo home. You are worth $11 million."

Chris high fived Robert. He said, "Robert, when you think we will get our money?"

Robert replied to everyone by saying, "Everyone, your attention please. Chris asked a wonderful question. He asked when will we get our money. Paige called the lottery hotline and told them we had the winning ticket. The lottery gaming corporation wanted to set up a TV conference and hand us all our checks. It will be this Friday morning at ten. We have to be patient for four more days. The good thing is that you have four days to plan your retirement. This will be the world's largest lottery ever."

Robert heard Paige and a couple others saying there were seven trainees that were not in the lottery pool. Robert needed to be sure they were online to take over the work load once the winners get the checks. Those seven people—plus the twenty or so that didn't participate in the lottery pool—would be enough to handle all the work orders. It appeared that restructuring would take place soon at Ianova Industries—and most people weren't pulling their weight in the drawing department. The people quitting because of winning the lottery is not really that big of a deal.

Paige asks Robert, "Are you going to quit?" "Ya right"

"My dad owns this place. I can't quit—he'll kill me. His dream is to leave this company behind for me."

"Oh well," said Paige. "We will all come to visit."

"What will you do with your winnings Paige?"

"What everyone dreams about. I will buy myself a nice home, a nice car, go on a dream vacation, and relax. How about you, Andrea? What will you do with your winnings?"

"I also will take a nice trip for a month. I will go to Greece and tour the islands. I will hire a gorgeous guy to take me on personal tours. He must be gorgeous—and he can have his way with me after we get married of course. I'll tell him to start slow and use his imagination. Then I will come back home after reflecting on my life with my new gorgeous husband and what I should do with the money. I will know then what to do. But until then, I will simply put my money in a bank account where it should be safe and determine what to do afterward."

Everyone giggles a little at Andrea's dream.

Paige turned up the radio and yelled, "Listen, everyone!

"It was firm, folks. There is a group of twenty-five happy people working at Ianova Industries that confirmed that they are in ownership of the world's largest lottery winning ticket in the history of lottery winnings. It was $275 million divided by twenty-five people. Each winner will take home $11 million. Not a bad payday. We will see their smiley faces this Friday at Ianova Industries where a check payable to each winner will be presented. Wow, great future to you folks."

Everyone was ecstatic because the winnings were sounding more and more real.

"Tim, what will you do with your winnings?" asked Paige.

"I will build my house. It will be custom. I will have remote things coming down from walls. I want weird stuff like off-the-wall colors. Also, I'll help my parents with their mortgage and stuff like that."

"How about you, Robert? What will you do?"

"I'll buy a Dodge Viper. I'll probably help my dad with this company a little more."

Tony Tuscony, Blair Hinder, Tim Timberlake, Josh Kaychuck, Julie Grey, Carrie Turner, Janet Brooke, Vito Vittorio, Nick De La Rokos, Ellen Wolfe, Dana Carriage, and Teneal Taylor wanted to plan a trip to Arizona to walk around the desert and Grand Canyon. Tony, Blair, and Tim would book the tickets and all of them wanted to take the trip before they got their winning payout because they couldn't wait.

Leah walked in and said, "Look at all the smiley faces. You'd think you guys won the lottery or something."

Everyone who was left laughed.

Leah walked around and congratulated everyone on their winnings. She walked up to Andrea and asked, "Are you going to go to Greece like you always dreamed?"

"I will, Mrs. Ianova. It has been a dream that I could never afford, but now that I can afford it, I have to go. I hope it is as pretty as all the pictures you showed me when you guys went there."

"It will be. Even prettier, pictures do not do justice to the real view you get when you are there. Do everything you want, Andrea. We really enjoyed you working here."

"You are talking like I quit, Mrs. Ianova."

"I took it for granted that you would quit."

"Mrs. Ianova, without purpose or hope, we have nothing. Without a job, what purpose or hope is there in life? Why would I quit?"

"I understand that with a job you have purpose, but what hope could you attain?"

"The hope that I am a good person, that people love me for who I am, the hope I do a great job, the hope that you and Mr. Ianova see and realize and acknowledge that I do a great job, the hope I can have a family as great as yours."

Leah reached out and embraced Andrea. They hugged each other tightly.

"You are a wonderful person, and people do love you. Your hope was answered because Mr. Ianova and I do acknowledge your work and you for who you are. You are more than welcome to stay in your position. We at Ianova Industries are more than happy to keep you forever."

"Great. I will be here forever."

They both turned and walked away. Leah congratulated Tim on his winnings. He looked down; he was shy in one-on-one conversations with women.

She asked, "What will you do with your winnings?"

He said, "Nothing. I will wait and see. Bye, Mrs. Ianova."

Leah laughed as she knew Tim was shy and a man of few words. The cleaning crew was called in to clean the party leftovers.

Leah looked at the mess and said, "God help this company. What went so wrong?"

Andrea walked up to Tim and Robert and asked, "You guys want to go out and grab a coffee or a drink somewhere?"

Robert said, "I'm too young to drink, and I don't feel like a coffee. Besides, I think I'd better stick around as my dad had a few important meetings today with suppliers and bankers. If I'm not here and my dad needs me for something, he'll get pretty mad if he finds out that Elvis has left the building."

Tim and Andrea both laughed. Tim was too shy to go alone with Andrea but agreed to go. Tim stared at Andrea because she was so pretty; he couldn't believe he would have coffee or a drink with her. He was scared stiff and probably wouldn't say a word or contribute to the conversation. Leah was at the other end of the office.

"Mrs. Ianova, do you want to join Tim and I for a coffee and desert or something?"

Leah smiled. "Thanks for the offer, but I will stick around here. We have a lot of work to do, and I really need to be here. But let's do it another time for sure. Ask me again soon."

Leah walked up to Robert and asked if he knew why there was a bloodstain on the floor.

Robert raised his bloodied fist and said, "It was Paul Lazarus's blood."

Robert explained that Paul had disrespected his Grandma, and he wasn't going to take it. He said Paul had a bad attitude about the mistakes he was making around the office and rubbed him the wrong way.

"You should have seen Paige, Mom. She walked up and kicked Paul twice while he was on the ground. She hates Paul. I didn't even realize that."

"Paige did that? Wow, I always pictured Paige as a tame little girl.

I guess you really can't judge a book by its cover."

"I had to stop her, Mom. She was going to keep kicking Paul. I actually started to feel sorry a bit for Paul."

Leah laughed because she couldn't believe what Paige had done. Leah wiped the smirk off her face and said, "Robert, what have we taught you all these years?"

"I know, Mom. Violence offers no cure, and fighting solves nothing. I was wondering when you were going to ask me that."

"I love you, son."

"I love you too, Mom."

CHAPTER 7

Meeting with Suppliers

"Mr. Ianova, Leval Preston of Tech Hardware, Adam Wendell of Stain Refinishers, Ventres Hullman of Cantrac Systems, Frank Ianetti of North American Truck Lines, Pierce Tredline of Woodboard, and Spiro Meeles of Draw Computer Services are all here to see you, sir."

"Well, here it goes, Dune. Send them all into the boardroom."

Vanity showed all the gentlemen to Ian's boardroom. They all got comfortably seated.

Ian and Dune walk into the room. Ian introduced Dune as the new controller. Ian knew everyone very well as he had done business with all of them for decades. Ian started off by thanking them all for coming—and for the years of support.

Frank said, "Ian, we are all here for a reason. Ianova Industries is in big trouble. The word on the street is that you will go into Chapter 11 and screw your suppliers. Quite frankly, you mismanaged this company—and all of us here will suffer because of it. You owe my company three months of unpaid invoices. I want to know—and everyone here wants to know—when are we getting paid?"

"I have a plan—"

Pierce Tredline cut off Ian. He said, "Ian, we have been business associates for over twenty years. We have unpaid invoices for four months. Ben has not returned our calls. You have not returned our calls."

"I was away," said Ian.

Pierce said, "Oh, you had a nice vacation?"

"It was business."

"Where was business, Ian?"

"Palm Springs, California?."

"Were you golfing at all on this business trip?"

"Look, Pierce—"

"No. You look, Ian. Four months of unpaid invoices is bad news. I can't operate my company this way. I put you on COD this morning. It will be that way until I see some money."

"Pierce, you can't do that to me."

"What? I can't do that to you? Are you friggin' nuts?"

"You owe me millions, you fool."

"You alone can bankrupt my company. Any idea how that sits with me? Please—"

"We have known each other for years; how can you screw a friend? Ian, I have the same question for you—how can you screw a friend? What will you do to make this right? You are screwing me, you are screwing us."

"I have a meeting with the bankers later today. We will have a game plan by morning for all of you."

"Okay. That means I am wasting my time here. You called this meeting for what? I have things to do. I have a company to try to keep profitable—even though you owe me millions in unpaid invoices. You called us all in for a mockery session! You have no information as to how we are all going to get paid, do you?"

"No. I don't," said Ian.

"Then quit wasting my time until you do. It's all over the news. Your son was one of the winners of the big lottery. Why not use his share of the winnings to pay some of us?"

"It's not my money."

"He is your son; he'll do whatever you ask him to do—but only if you ask him to." Pierce walked out.

Frank said, "You still didn't answer my question. When am I getting paid?"

"I don't know."

"You're on COD until you do know." Frank walked out.

Adam said, "Ian, I have the same problem as all the gentlemen you called in here this morning. My company is not a big company; my business is about $15 million annual. Almost 80 percent of my business is with Ianova Industries. I have ten other clients I supply, but you're the biggest. My operating line is maxed out, and I can't afford to pay the interest on it. Ian, you will bankrupt my company if you don't pay me. So many cents on the dollar won't cut it either if you go Chapter 11. I need full payment to survive."

"Why are you and the others talking to me about Chapter 11? That never came into play with me."

"Wherever there is smoke, there is fire Ian. Gossip more often than not becomes reality eventually. I will sue you personally for breach of trust and misappropriated funds if I have to in order to protect my company."

Adam began to head toward the doorway.

Ian said, "Wait, Adam. Come on, we have known each other for years. Don't abandon me when I am in trouble."

"You abandoned me, Ian."

Ventres said, "Hey Adam, why go alone? Let's go class action so we save a little bit of money on lawyers when we sue this guy. I'm with you on the lawsuit."

"Okay," said Adam.

Adam and Ventres walked out. Only Dune, Ian, and Spiro remained in the office.

Vanity paged Ian over the intercom.

Ian said, "Not now, Vanity."

"I think you want to hear this, Ian. Please pick up the phone."

"What is it, Vanity?"

"The police phoned and said that Paul Lazarus, Chris, John, and Phil Epson all died in a car crash."

"Oh no. Why would the police call us about that? How would they even know they worked here?"

"The cop at the scene was Glen Heron, your buddy. He called because he recognized the car that Paul drove from seeing it in our parking lot. He said the bodies were unrecognizable."

"Oh my Goodness," said Ian. "Call any florist and get flowers to all the families involved here. Send it tomorrow—not today. I'd hate for flowers to arrive before the news was broken to the respective families. E-mail all employees about the tragedy. Thank you, Vanity."

"Okay, sir."

"What happened?" asked Spiro.

"I heard that four of my workers from the work order department just had a collision—and all of them died."

"Ex-workers," said Dune.

Spiro said, "What do you mean ex-workers?"

Dune said, "We were trying to clean house here and get rid of any dead wood."

"That was not funny at all," said Spiro.

"Oh my Goodness," said Dune. "I was not trying to be funny at all in the remotest of ways. It was simply a business expression when trying to clean up."

"Stop," said Spiro. "I know what it means—and I know the innuendo. This company is in financial trouble; it's reminiscent of who runs this company. Things are said in poor taste, in poor context and completely mismanaged."

Ian said, "Spiro, come on. That was unfair. Dune is new here. It's his first day. Please cut him some slack. He had no beef with the people that were fired this morning. He doesn't even know them."

"That's my point, Ian. Think before you speak because you offend someone. Then that someone may kill you."

"What are you saying, Spiro? What are you talking about? You make no sense. What are you talking about killings for? You're scaring me, Spiro. Are you okay?"

"No. I'm not okay. My company is on the verge of bankruptcy because of you. I feel like killing myself—that's what I mean."

"Dune, do we have anything on hand that we can cut Spiro a check for?"

"No, sir. We don't," said Dune.

Ian asked, "You mean we don't even have a grand in the bank?"

Dune said, "Without a favorable outcome from this afternoon's meeting with the bankers, sir, we won't even make payroll."

"Oh for the love of"

"You are in so much crap here, Ian, that you don't even know how deep into it you are. That is scarier than anything I heard here so far this morning. Call me this afternoon—after your meeting. I want to know what is happening. If you want me to settle on so many cents on the dollar, I'm going to join Adam and Ventres in the class action lawsuit. I'll tell you something else, Ian, I will push as hard as I can to get all your suppliers into the lawsuit. At least we'll save a little on lawyers instead of all of us going at it alone. From what I am hearing, you're going Chapter 11."

Spiro walked out.

Ian shook his head in disbelief. He looked at Dune and said, "You went through all the books here. What the heck went wrong?"

"It's simple, Ian. The exchange rate killed you, and you did nothing about it. You sold jobs at cost—and even less than cost—and relied on profit from the exchange rate. You never counted on errors. You did not price thinking you would make an error on projects. You had nothing in your contract for protection either."

"Like what?"

"Like exchange rate escalation."

"What's that?"

"It's a clause in your contract that protects you from exchange rate fluctuations that do not turn in your favor. In other words, if the rate drops like it did in this case, your clause would protect you from that."

"Come on, Dune. My customers wouldn't agree to that."

"Maybe they won't entirely, but more than likely they would have agreed to split it with you. But now you have nothing. Also, your contracts had no time limit attached. In other words, if a project was late for a year for some reason or another, you kept your same price with no price escalation, which was real dumb. If your suppliers increased their prices to you, you ate it without passing it on to your customers. Almost all your contracts were over one year old and almost every supplier increased their rates to you. You were eating the 17 percent exchange rate difference and a 5-7 percent supplier increase. Your total loss was over 20 percent on projects you signed up with 5-10 percent margins. Your operating line was maxed out, and you had 7 percent interest to pay on that line. That put you at almost a 30 percent total loss of revenue."

"Dune, are you telling me I should go bankrupt?"

"It seems that is the direction we need to go. Think about it, Ian. You've made no changes in the factory, production costs are the same, and you're losing money daily. You can't fix your problems fast enough here."

Mrs. Ianova walked in and said, "Is it true what Barbara was saying to me, dear? You're going to file for Chapter 11?"

"No, honey. We are not. I am having a meeting with the bankers this afternoon, and we will fix everything. Please let me handle this."

Barbara walks in and says, "Your meeting this afternoon with the bankers is to talk about how you will restructure the company—the plant operations, the way we buy from suppliers, the hours of work, and the potential to get more work out of less staff."

"What are you talking about, Mom? How can I do that on such short notice? I made the meeting and chose the topic for discussion."

"Sorry, son. Your topic for discussion was the same as the way you let this company go. Full of nonsense. You need a game plan—and you don't have one. Dune, did you know about all of this since my mom put you in position?"

"Yes. I did, sir. I guess all the paperwork you prepared was also for the bankers and outlines a plan for Chapter 11, doesn't it?"

"Yes it does sir—and with some changes that will be implemented, we will emerge from bankruptcy a better, leaner company."

"I can't believe you left me out of all this, Mom."

"Look at the state of the company, Ian. Would you leave it to yourself if you were me? The company slipped away through your fingers—and you didn't even know it. I should have faith in you, especially since you had no game plan as to how you can make this company financially sound again? Are you kidding me? What were you going to talk about with the bankers? Were you going to ask for a greater operating line of credit and extended terms? Do you think the bankers are fools? Do you really think they would give you a dime?" "Ian, I can't believe this is happening. I thought everything was going very well here."

"I suppose I thought so too, Leah. Sorry I let all of you down."

Ian walked out of the boardroom.

"Let's go grab a quick bite before the bankers get here," said Barbara.

CHAPTER 8

Meeting with Bankers

"Sir, Mr. Chad Gibbons and Mr. George Korokolis of World Bank are here to see you."

"Send them in. And send in Dune and my mother."

Dune, Chad, and George were laughing and joking like they already knew each other.

Ian said, "What is going on here? You guys are buddies already."

"Mr. Ianova, your mother said the bankers and Dune know what to do. She won't be joining you," said Vanity.

Ian maintained a smile so the others in his office couldn't tell how furious he was that he had been kept out of the loop. He said, "Good afternoon, good to see you again."

"Ian, let's make it simple for everyone. Explain to me what you have already decided. Your mother called us in four weeks ago to meet with her and Dune. She is the majority owner of Ianova Industries, and she swore us to secrecy. It was not our choice to meet her behind your back."

"Oh spare me the bull, Chad."

George said, "Ian, come on. You would do the same if you were in our shoes."

"Then why am I here? Years of business with me clearly meant nothing. Why am I in this office?"

George said, "It doesn't matter what we would have done. We were always in a loose situation. We had a task to perform, your mother said you were on board, and we need to perform this task. Perhaps I was misinformed; are you on board to run this company or do we need to get Barbara back in here? You tell us what to do."

Ian took fifteen seconds. "Okay. What is the plan to get this company back into the black? Let's talk."

Dune said, "The long and the short is we need to go into Chapter 11."

Ian said, "Next! That is not an option."

George said, "Ian, it's Chapter 11—not Chapter 7. Do you know the difference?"

"Yes. Chapter 11 is going bankrupt."

"No it's not. It's restructuring and renegotiating with your bank and your suppliers while still performing day-to-day business as normal. Chapter 7 is going bankrupt where you close your doors and dissolve the company. We are here to help you make a deal with your suppliers so you can pay them what is fair under the circumstances that we are in."

Ian said, "The suppliers will not agree that what we deem as fair to them. Dune, you heard Adam, Spiro, and Ventris this morning. They will get together and form a class action lawsuit against us if we even think of not paying them what we owe."

George said, "Ian, a court-approved judge will oversee our moves and our offers to be sure that what we do—that what we say is fair. The courts will see the financial position that you are in, and they will know you have no money to pay the suppliers. The money offered is the money on hand to pay."

"What if the suppliers do not agree with our offer?"

"If they don't take your offer, they will have the option to sue you. If they feel your company is worth more than what you are offering them, they can take over the company and sell if off piece by piece. The offer we present to the suppliers really needs to be a fair offer. It needs to be the same for everyone. It means that you offer Spiro fifty cents on the dollar. You cannot offer Adam seventy-five cents on the dollar and Ventris sixty-cents on the dollar. The offer needs to be the same across the board for everyone."

"I will loose a lot of confidence from the years of business I had with these guys—as well as the friendships that I had developed with them."

George said, "It's better than closing the doors of the business your daddy started, isn't it?"

"Yeah. I guess so. How about my employees? If we have no money for payroll, and it is business as usual, how are they looked after?"

George replied, "They will be on our payroll under Chapter 11 protection as of tomorrow. They will all get paid as if nothing ever happened. We'll have to disperse a letter to all your employees tomorrow morning indicating what we are doing because rumors will get out. You want to squash those ASAP."

"Okay. What is the proposal?"

"We offer fifty cents on the dollar. That will put you far ahead of the game. It will put you into the black again, and you really need to restructure the factory. You need to administer layoffs where possible. You need to become a more streamlined company and make people in responsible positions report to you on the status of their departments. That makes the responsible people in positions more aware of their position and more aware of not making errors because they will realize that you are watching them. And you don't really have to read each and every line on the report your supervisors will give you because you will be able to read between the lines and figure out what is happening. You will be surprised by how this company will turn around when you implement these things—even in a market where the dollar is not in your favor."

"Where do we go from here? How is this handled? Your mother already hired her own lawyer. Her name is Train Ramsyer. Train describes how she operates. She comes at you like a freight train."

Train walked in and said, "Wow, Dune, I didn't think you thought of me as a freight train. I don't know if I should feel happy or sad about that nickname. How do you do, Ian? I hope you don't mind me calling you Ian instead of Mr. Ianova."

"I prefer Mr. Ianova." says Ian with a smirck on his face.

"Great. Sure, Ian it is then." She was flexing her muscles and showing no sign of intimidation.

"Sit down, Train. I hope you don't me calling you Train," said Ian.

"Ms. Ramsyer will be fine, Ian."

"Great, Train it is then." Ian says with that same smirck.

"Yes, Ian I do mind actually. You need to refer to me as Ms. Ramsyer. Thank you very much. I'm kidding, Ian. It's great to know that you can't tell when I am joking. That will surely come in handy one day. Sure, you can call me Train."

Ian's face lit up. He swiped his forehead and said, "Whew, you really do come on like a train. I feel sorry for our suppliers."

"I will take that as a compliment."

"I asked Dune if you were good. I need to know that you are on my side. My side is to be fair to this company and fair to my suppliers."

Train said, "There are a lot of people out there that you are going to piss off with this offer. The only fair thing the suppliers think is to be paid 100 percent of what you owe them. That's fair to them and unfair to you. Pay the suppliers twenty-five cents on the dollar, and that is unfair to them and great for you. Pay them fifty cents on the dollar, and that is somewhat fair to them and somewhat fair to you—even though they won't see it that way. What this offer will do is maintain jobs here at Ianova Industries and at your suppliers' businesses. The other benefit is that your suppliers most likely will rebuild their companies, trim their own fat, and become better, more streamlined, and profitable companies like Ianova Industries will become. It's a win-win situation for everyone—even though the suppliers will not see it that way initially."

"Okay. I believe you, but I feel that I will be screwing the same people who made me successful in the first place. How can I do that to them?"

"You need to learn that business has its ups and downs with good times and bad times. All good things must come to an end, Ian. A good job got shattered because of company scale backs, a loved one was lost because of old age, a house was foreclosed because a mortgage payment wasn't made—even a good marriage was dissolved because of infidelity."

"I get the point, Train. You don't need to go into all that stuff."

"Next time, Ian, don't ask me how so I don't have to waste my time and explain it to you if you already know how."

"Wow, O'k, easy Train. What's next?"

"I have a letter ready to go out to your suppliers. Sign this consent form; the letters will detail the structure of settlement for them. Either do it or close your doors. I can take your keys and wind down this company as well as help you restructure. I do both. I want to see this company turned around, you do have a great company here, I would not like to see it closed down. However, it's your choice."

"I thought my mother already made this choice."

"Your mother laid the groundwork because she knew you had a soft heart and needed logical convincing. She wanted the final approval to come from you because she knew you would do the right thing to keep this company going strong and establish profitability once again."

"Let's do it."

"Okay. Sign here; the letters will go out in one hour by courier. Gentlemen, I have work to do—and you have work to do. Good day."

"Train, thanks for your help."

Train exited the room.

"Vanity, is there any other word from Glen about the car accident?"

"No, sir. The police are still investigating."

"Call me if you hear any news."

Barbara walked in with Leah. "Was that really bad, son?"

"I guess not. I am really concerned how all the suppliers will handle what we do."

"Ian, it's better than closing our doors. And at the rate we were heading, closing the doors is the direction we were going in. It's okay, Ian. All we have can't be touched—our cars, our homes, nothing. So restructure this company, and we will all be fine."

"Some suppliers were talking about class action lawsuits and going after me personally. Can they do that? Can they sue us personally?"

"No," said Barbara and Dune almost in unison. "Unless they can prove Ian that you squandered the suppliers' money before paying them and then treated yourself to expensive material purchases."

"I bought a place in France last month," said Ian.

"Why?" asked Barbara.

"I wanted to surprise Leah for our anniversary because she loves France. I thought we were doing great based on our last financials. Until a few days ago, I didn't know we were in so much financial turmoil."

"Honey, I can't believe you did that for me."

Barbara said, "I can't believe that you did that either. How much did you spend?"

"Six million."

"That's great," said Barbara.

Leah hugged Ian, and she is wearing a loving smile from cheek to cheek.

Dune said, "If the suppliers don't accept our deal, then you will be in trouble because if they do go class action, your purchase will be picked up and then all hell will break loose. You will be scrutinized to the penny for the last six months."

"Why six months?"

"Because you could have planned this restructuring since your last profitable financial statement because you noticed the exchange rate turning from your favor. You heard Ben. He tried doing things his way, he saw the rate changing, he knew it, and quite frankly, you should have as well. The courts will also agree that you, as owner, should have been aware of the state of the world's economy. Imagine how they will think. You should have known the state of your own local economy, especially the exchange rates, since that determines profitability or losses for your company."

"I bought two Escalades as well—one for me and one for Leah."

"That's small stuff," said Dune. "The courts will look at big expenses."

"I paid off the company jet two months ago."

"How much was that?"

"That was five million."

Barbara said, "Great. That's $11 million within six months.

Dune said, "Okay, let's work hard with suppliers to get them to agree to fifty cents on the buck. By the way Ian, why are you asking about the cops?" "Paul, Chris, John and Phil have all died in a car crash." "What" asks Barbara and Leah in unison? "Oh my" says Dune. "Glen phoned and said they were involved in a car accident" replies Ian. "I was just talking to all of them just like, 5 or 6 hours ago. What happened, what does Glen know? And let's send flowers out to their families" says Leah as she is starting to cry along with Barbara. "I have no details as yet and yes I have asked for flowers to go out tomorrow" says Ian. "Tomorrow, why tomorrow?" Because we don't want flowers arriving before the police notifies the families honey. Come on, It's been a long, hard day. Let's all go home now," says Ian.

CHAPTER 9

Suspicions

As was a daily practice, work orders were brought into the production office for three weeks down the road for production. This way, the ordering took place and everything got delivered to the job site on time. It was a system that worked as long as the buyer started his job in purchasing product on time.

Liz Dunshap and Margo Sanchez ran the documentation up into the production office. They talked about not being able to wait until Friday to get their checks from the lottery. They joked about the news conference because they both felt they would be famous and they would have their choice of good-looking, tall, muscular men.

Liz and Margo were at the production plant. They walked through a small portion of the production plant in order to get to the production office. It was relatively dark, but the sun had not set. Margo asked Liz if she knew where the lights were.

Liz said, "Yes, I do, but it doesn't matter. The lights take ten minutes to light up, they are those fancy sun lights that are cheap to run and brighten everything up, and we will be there for only a few minutes tops."

Margo said, "Good to know. It's funny. I worked here for years and never knew that. Every time I came to work, the lights were always on."

Liz brought drawings to Albert, and Margo came along for the company. Liz and Margo heard an air gun shooting staples. They heard two or three shots. They knew the sound because they used to be assemblers, and some of their coworkers used to play a game and shoot staples at each other. They both giggled because it was a lot of fun.

Liz yelled, "Who is shooting? Show yourself. Margo and I will kick your butts. Be sure to have your goggles on because I will aim for your eyes."

Margo and Liz started laughing. A few more shots are fired. A few more again!

"Sure, shoot us when we were defenceless? No fair. Who is there?"

Liz yelled, "Come on, coward. Show yourself. We want to play too."

She was more afraid than Margo. More staples shot toward them. Liz at this point was freaking out! She turned and ran toward the production office while Margo stood outside of the office door. She opened the office door, slammed the production copies on the desk, ran out, and grabbed Margo's arm to get out of the production facilities.

She heard the staple fire again and yelled, "It's not funny!"

They started running, but a tall section of cabinets fell over and landed on top of Liz and Margo. They were both screaming. They were both trapped. Liz's leg was bent in a position that legs don't normally sit in. She had blood all over her face and arms. There was no sound at all from Margo.

Liz said, "Margo, are you okay?"

There was no answer, Margo was motionless.

Liz screamed, "Help! Please someone help me. I can't move. My leg is broken." She heard footsteps coming toward her, she saw a face, and said, "Oh it's you. Thank Goodness These cabinets fell on Margo and me. I think they weren't stacked properly. Can you please call 911?"

"Margo?"

Liz replied, "I think Margo is dead. She is right over there. Hey, by the way, what are you doing here now, the plant is supposed to be closed?"

All of a sudden, "no, no, please no" yells Liz" Puff, a swing like a baseball bat to Liz's head with a piece of cabinetry just took place. Liz's head went flying back and she died. You can see the footsteps walking away from the scene as Liz's face looks battered and so does Margo's.

Ian and his family were at home talking about the day's events. Ian was worried about what would happen when the suppliers found out about the offer. Spiro had called and left three messages. Ian had promised Spiro that he would get back to him later in the day but never had.

Ian said, "That was one guy who has lost respect for me already."

Leah said, "How can you say that?"

Robert said, "Yeah, Dad. You and Spiro go way back.

Ian said, "That's right, son. We do go way back. I should have called and told him what this company was doing."

Barbara said, "Ian, it's tough times. If you and your suppliers really are great friends, then they will understand."

"I hope so. I'm tired, folks. I'm going to bed. Goodnight to all."

In the morning, Albert was the first guy to the production area. He saw the fallen cabinetry. He shook his head in disbelief. He went into his office and noticed the production copies and reviewed them until two of his employees came in.

Sheko Chamber and Sam Gunner had been plant lead hands for a few years.

Albert said, "Sheko, Sam, get a bunch of laborers together and clean up the mess outside. Separate what we can use again from the trash."

Sheko and Sam waited twenty minutes for a bunch of guys to come in and make their way toward the fallen cabinetry. Sam pointed to the problem area and started giving instructions to the laborers. He noticed Liz. "Oh my God. Look at this, Sheko."

Sheko noticed Margo and said, "Sam, look at this, another person."

"Holy crap," said Sam. "Liz and Margo were from the work order department."

Sam and Sheko walked fast to Albert's office and told him what they had seen. Albert picked up the phone and called 911. He called Ian's cell phone and told him what his boys had seen.

Ian said, "Okay. I'll be right there." Ian got out of bed.

Leah said, "Ian, where are you going so early?"

"To the office, honey. There was a terrible accident. Margo and Liz are dead. Cabinets fell on top of them in the plant."

"Oh my Goodness," said Leah. "I'm coming with you."

"No. I'm leaving. I will keep you informed."

Ian got ready and started driving to his office. He called Glen and told him what was happening. Glen said 911 had already called him; he was on his way to the plant.

"Okay, great," replied Ian. "I'll see you there in ten minutes."

As Ian pulled up into his plant, RDE.TV was already there—as well 911 emergency units and a few police cars. Ian got out of his car and was greeted almost instantly by a question from the media, "Mr. Ianova, what do you make out of all these killings in light of your son's lottery winnings?"

"What the heck are you talking about? What killings?"

"Isn't it strange, sir, that six people are dead—all of whom had a share in the largest lottery winning ever?"

"There were twenty-five winners," replied Ian. "I don't know what you're talking about."

"Sir, if you do the math, taking away six people leaves nineteen people to split the money. A greater amount—almost $3.5 million more—for you."

"I don't know what you are talking about! My tickets didn't win."

"Yes, but your son's did."

"You guys know more about this than me obviously." Ian tried to push his way through the circus outside his office.

"Is your company going bankrupt, Mr. Ianova? Is that why you had these killings orchestrated?"

Ian stopped dead in his tracks, turned, and asked, "Who said that?" No one answered; in fact, there was silence. "Who said that? I want to know who said that." He walked slowly into the crowd.

A young lady asked, "Why do you want to know who said something out of free speech, sir? So you can kill them?" Her name tag read Gail Sclarz.

"No, Gail. I don't want to kill them. I want to know what is happening here." He walked back into his building visibly upset.

As soon as Ian walked into the building, an officer told Ian that Glen was waiting for him up at the production area. Ian walked at a very fast pace and saw people bent over the bodies, a pool of blood, and what looked like toolboxes with special apparatuses being used to take samples. He couldn't believe what he saw. He looked at Glen and Albert standing together and walked over.

"Albert what the heck happened here?"

Albert said, "It appears that the cabinets fell on top of the girls."

Ian said, "I can see that. How did that happen?"

Glen said, "We'll investigate that, and we will find out. We need to shut the plant down for a day or so while we investigate."

"I can't shut this place down. I have orders to fill."

Glen said, "No choice, Ian. It needs to happen while we investigate. That car crash was no accident either my friend—someone loosened the car's steering linkages. That's why they went into the opposing traffic and had a head-on collision."

Ian said, "Maybe he was on his cell phone, wasn't paying attention to his driving, maybe he was texting then drifted into opposing traffic, had the crash, and the impact loosened the linkages. Maybe that's how it happened."

"Maybe it happened that way Ian,—and maybe not. That's why we are investigating that crash and this incident. Also, your son had a fight with Paul; did you know that?"

"No. I didn't. What kind of fight."

"It was a fist fight, Ian."

"How do you know?" asked Ian.

"Some of the work order staff phoned our hotline to tell us after they heard about the car crash."

"Is my son being investigated, Glen?"

"We are not leaving any stone unturned," said Glen.

"I don't believe you. You knew us before Robert was even born. How could you even remotely think he had anything to do with any of this? In all my years as a police detective, I learned one thing—money is the root of all evil. People do what they normally would never do unless they had eleven million reasons to. Lottery rules say that people must be able to accept the prize. If you are dead, you can't accept the prize. The difference left over in the lottery pot goes to the living people. You understand the predicament?"

"I understand you are investigating us—and the *killer* is out there. That is what I understand."

Glen said, "You're right, we have known each other since well before Robert was born—so let me do my job. If Robert is innocent, we will find that out, but please remove yourself from this location. There is a police investigation going on here."

"It's going to be like that is it Glen?"

"At this point Ian, you and Robert, don't leave town; we may need to speak to you both."

Ian walked away and his cell phone rang.

"Dad, it's Robert. What is happening there? I hear all kinds of things in the news."

"Robert, you never told me about the fight you had with Paul."

"What's the big deal?"

"Apparently you are being investigated because he and three others are dead. Margo and Liz were found dead at the plant. The police are investigating. They suspect you, son."

"I didn't hurt anyone, Dad."

"I know that son. We'll fix that real soon—don't worry. Hurry and get to work, Robert."

There is a car chase with Peter and Bill Bixby. The brothers work in the work order department. They are driving on a secluded part of Lake Drive.

Peter looked into his rear-view mirror and yelled, "Bill! Holy crap, man. This guy is going to ram us!"

Bill turned his head as a huge bang pushed the car forward.

"Peter, step on it. Get away from this jerk."

Peter was uncomfortable with the high speed. He yelled, "That corner is too sharp. I will lose it there."

Bill yelled, "Keep your foot into it, man!"

They were nailed again from behind; the car spun out three times. When the dust settled, they had stopped about ten feet from a forty-foot drop. They looked at each other and were stunned, but then a smile appeared on both of them.

"Bill, we do have horseshoes up our butts. We win the lottery—and then we escape some lunatic's driving as if he wanted to kill us or something. Let's go buy more lottery tickets before we get to the office. We'll win for sure." They both sigh and laugh in relief.

"That sounds like a plan. Stop for coffee. I need it."

Peter looked at the vehicle coming back to nail them again. He gunned the pedal to the floor, but the front tires were spinning and had no traction. He could not get out of the way.

"Bill, start praying. oh God please help us"

They got nailed and were pushed over the edge. The car landed and exploded, bouncing a few times first. No one could survive that explosion—let alone the impact.

An anonymous caller phoned 911 to report the incident. The 911 call center dispatched fire trucks, ambulances, and police to the scene. The police identified the plates and ran them. They also identified the driver and the passenger.

Glen Heron was still investigating the plant accident when he got a call telling him about the car accident and how it happened.

Glen replied, "Let me guess—on Lake Drive, correct?"

"Yes."

"How did you know that?"

"No other area has a small cliff as described to me except Lake Drive. Who owns the car?"

"After running the plates, it belongs to Mr. Peter Bixby, sir. It appears that Peter was the driver of the vehicle."

"Anyone else in the car?"

"Yes, sir. His brother Bill."

"Thanks," replied Glen.

Glen was en route to Ian's office. Pierce, Spiro, and Frank were also in the main office. Ian walked out of his office and ran into them in the main office.

"Good morning, gentlemen," said Ian.

Spiro said, "Forget good morning, Ian. You were to call yesterday after your banker meeting to tell us all how we were to get paid. You insisted Chapter 11 was out of the discussions, but you didn't call with good news."

Frank said, "What's up with that, Ian?"

Pierce said, "You're filing for Chapter 11. Aren't you? That's why no response, correct?"

"Yes, that's correct. We are filing for Chapter 11. You will all get letters today."

"That's great," said Pierce.

Ian said, "I can restructure, make a deal with you guys, or close my doors—and we all get nothing."

Pierce said, "As long as I know you get nothing, I'd rather see your company close."

Spiro asked, "What's the offer?"

"Fifty cents on the dollar."

There was no response from anyone other than heads shaking. Pierce, Spiro, and Frank walked out.

CHAPTER 10

Investigations Continue

Glen said, "Ian, I overheard your conversation with Frank, Spiro, and Pierce regarding the stain problem you have. Sorry to hear about what's going on."

"Yeah, I'm sorry too. What is it, Glen? What can I do for you?"

"Do you know Peter and Bill Bixby?"

"Yes. They work for me in the work order department. Why do you ask?"

"Where is Robert?"

"Why?"

"Because there was another car crash. Peter and Bill are dead. Your workers are dead. I ask you again, where is Robert?"

"He was en route here."

"All the other workers were here at the time of the crash. Why is he late?"

"I don't know," replied Ian. "Why don't you ask him yourself?"

Glen said, "I will, Ian. Were they also part of the group that won the lottery?"

"I don't know."

"Call Robert from your cell to see if he answers."

Ian got his cell and called Robert.

"You're late, son. Why?"

"There was some kind of accident on Lake Drive. We were rerouted, and I got held up in the traffic. I'll be there in less than ten minutes."

"Okay. I'll see you when you get here."

"Ask Robert if Peter and Bill were lottery winners."

"Robert, were Peter and Bill Bixby part of the lottery group?"

"Yes, they were. Why?"

Ian looked as though someone had just rung his bell as he realized the major coincidence. Another lottery death that his son could have orchestrated.

"Just wondering, Robert," replied Ian.

"Okay, Dad. Bye for now."

"Bye, son."

"He was held up in traffic because of the accident, and he was rerouted."

"Were they lottery winners or not?"

"They were."

"He is killing these people so he can win as much money as possible to bail you out of bankruptcy."

Ian said, "I know you think my son is a murderer."

Glen started making his way to the car accident scene when he saw Robert driving into the parking lot. They rolled down their windows.

Glen said, "Good morning, Robert."

Robert said, "Good morning."

Robert asked, "How did the accident happen to Margo and Liz?"

Do you think I'll tell you how our investigations are going so you will be a step ahead of us? Not in your dreams, buddy. "We are still investigating. We don't know anything yet, but we'll have answers in a day or so."

"Gotta find out what it was so it doesn't happen again," said Robert.

"You're right, that certainly is the intention. Got to go, Robert. We'll see you soon."

"Okay, sir. Take care."

Glen took a detour because the emergency vehicles were still blocking a lot of the roadway. In a driveway of an abandoned house, a Ford F-150 has caught the attention of Glen. He notices that it has front end damage. He pulled over and looked closer. The home was boarded up. No residents for sure. Glen pulled over toward the truck. He felt the hood. *This was parked here within the hour; it's still hot.*

Glen radioed for an officer to come to where he was. Glen pulled out his gun and started walking around the house. It looked eerie and scary as he walked around, but he found nothing.

He heard a noise. He approached the area with great caution; his gun was pointed directly at a corner he was about to turn.

He yelled, "Don't move!"

"Don't shoot me, sir," replied an officer. "Sergeant Hans Prague asked me to come here to see you."

"Sorry, Officer Hady. It's been a bad morning."

"I can imagine, sir."

"Look at the truck. Tell me what you make out of it."

They walked together to the front. Stan looked at the truck and saw the front-end damage. He noticed it was hot. He noticed a blue color on the truck's bumper.

"This is strange. This vehicle was parked here about an hour ago, and this color blue here on the bumper has an uncanny resemblance to the car that went over the cliff this morning."

"Do you think this truck forced the car over the edge?"

"It's too early to say, but it sure looks suspicious. Send a chip of this blue color to the lab to see if it matches the car that went over the cliff."

They walked toward the entrance to the driveway and noticed a small driveway off to the side. They noticed fresh tire tracks. A portion of the driveway was rather sandy and a very detailed portion showed a tire track.

"Stan, what if there is a killer—and this was no accident. The killer parked his vehicle here, left the area, and then stole this F-150. He knew the route Peter and Bill Bixby would take to work and waited for them to pass his little hiding spot. He followed them to the part of the roadway that had a cliff. He rams them once or twice and then forces them over the edge. What chance could that little car have against this truck? Run this truck's plate number. See if it was reported stolen."

Stan called dispatch. He said, "Run a plate number in for me—and tell me if anything comes back."

Glen said, "You want to bet these plates come back as stolen? I bet this blue paint matches the paint on the car over the cliff? I think we have a huge problem at Ianova Industries: Robert Ianova."

"Why would he kill anyone? He has everything imaginable."

"You're right, Stan, but what he doesn't have is a father with a thriving company like the days of old. Ianova Industries is going down."

Dispatch called and said the plate belonged to a 2006 Ford F-150. It had been reported stolen at midnight from 123 Pinnacle Avenue.

Glen said, "Stan, get me a report on the tire treads and the paint. I got to go."

Glen got back into his car and drove around the corner to the accident scene. He got out of his car and looked down at the fallen car of Peter and Bill. *Smooth move, Robert, but I will get you, you little punk.*

It hadn't taken long for RDE.TV to show up at the scene. Gail Sclarz slipped through with a cameraman and ran straight to Glen Heron.

"Glen, what can you tell us about this accident?"

"Come on, Gail. You know this is an investigation. What can I tell you that you can't see here for yourself? Look, there is a car down there, and there are two people dead that are in the car."

Gail asked, "Is there any connection between this car crash and the other one where four Ianova Industries employees lost their lives? They were all part of the big lottery pool winning, weren't they?"

"We don't know."

Gail asked, "Did the two dead guys in that car work for Ianova Industries?"

Glen said, "I can't answer that."

Gail said, "You just did."

Glen shook his head and drove back to Ianova Industries.

At Ianova Industries, it was determined by the investigating officers that a worn piece of support wood structure had collapsed, sending the supported cabinetry to its fall. Albert asked Sam Gunner to build a new foundation for a new support with double support beams in preparation for when the investigation was concluded.

Sam took some dimensions and headed over to the table saw with the materials. He turned on the table saw and the blade propelled right into Sam's heart. He screamed and fell to the ground. It was heard at the investigation area since they were very close to each other.

All who ran over to the table saw stared at Sam. He was on the ground, dead, with his eyes wide open. Glen was called and informed about what happened.

Glen said, "I'm pulling in. I will be there in two minutes." He pulled into the parking lot and ran into the front office.

Vanity called Ian and told him that Glen had returned.

Ian made his way over toward the production plant. Glen arrived at the scene and saw Sam in the pool of blood. He saw the saw blade in Sam's heart.

"What the heck happened here?"

Albert said, "I sent Sam here to cut the required material. Whoever replaced the last dull blade on the saw did not tighten the new blade properly. It was a freak accident."

"I thought I said that no more production was to take place until this investigation was closed."

"Glen, there was no production here. This was cutting material to strengthen the weak part of a support beam. No one was making cabinets here—look around you."

"Who last changed the saw blade here?"

"That was Sam's job," replied Albert. "He changed it himself. I guess he was a victim of his own doing."

Glen said, "Detective, get me prints on all the areas where a person needs to touch this machine in order to change the saw blades. Let me know what you come up with."

"Right away, sir," replied the detective.

CHAPTER 11

Pointed Questions

"Was Sam part of the pool that won the lottery?" asked Glen.

Everyone shrugged their shoulders; no one knew. Ian heard the conversation. Glen asked Ian to check with Robert to see if Sam was part of the lottery pool.

Ian said, "I don't like the innuendo, Glen."

"Why is Robert the dedicated lottery questioner person? Paige headed the lottery pool and got in touch with lottery headquarters about the winnings, and she set up the news conference this Friday so the group can get their checks live on TV. Why don't you question her?"

"Oh, I will. Don't worry about that. I thought you wanted to help in this investigation, that's all."

"I do, but Robert is not the go-to guy here."

Glen walked back into the reception area and asked to speak to Paige. Vanity called Paige and asked her to meet with Glen Heron in the boardroom. Vanity told Glen to head into the boardroom, and Paige would meet him there.

Glen walked into the boardroom and momentarily waited. He whispered, "Money sure is the root of all evil."

Paige made her way into the boardroom. She was all smiles as she walked into the boardroom.

Glen said, "What are you so smiley about?"

Paige replied, "You forgot? Three more days before I am holding the big check."

He said, "Oh, sorry, Paige. I forgot. I'm so focused on what I wanted to ask you. Of course, I'd be all smiles if I had a check your size coming my way."

"All you had to do was buy a ticket. You can't win unless you do. What can I do for you, Detective Heron?"

"Call me Glen."

"Okay."

"Do you have a list of the names in your pool?"

"Of course I do."

"I will need a copy of that list. Before you get it, do you know by memory who was in the pool."

"Of course I do. It's the same people every week. It is easy to remember who was in it. There were at least four other lottery pools within the company, and I'm sure all those people know who is in their pools as well."

"Okay, Paige. I'll need that list from you. Can you confirm that Paul, Chris, John, and Phil were on the list?"

"Yes, they were."

"Were Margo and Liz on the list?"

"Yes they were. Robert told me what happened to them; it was a terrible accident. I sure hope the plant will do what they need to in order to ensure this type of accident never happens again."

"Paige, how did the lottery corporation know who to make the checks payable to?"

"I gave them a list."

"Did you call the lottery corporation to take these six people off the list?"

"I did, Glen."

"Did the corporation ask you why you were taking six people from twenty-five off your original list?"

"No, they haven't."

"Were Sam, Bill, and Peter Bixby part of the lottery pool winners?"

"Yes, they are. And why are you referring to them as *were* like pastence?"

"Why are you doing that?"

"Because they are dead as well."

"Oh my God. What happened?"

"Sam had an accident with a piece of machinery in the plant, and Peter and Bill were murdered in a car accident."

"I can't believe that, murdered? That is incredible. I'll have to call the lottery corporation to tell them."

"How do you feel about getting more money in the wake of all these deaths?"

"I don't like that people are dying, but I love money."

"Do you realize that we are investigating all these deaths as murder investigations?"

"No. I thought they were all accidental."

"Accidentally suspicious, Paige—not true accidents."

"Wow. I had no idea."

"I need to get to my office to fill out a report so I will see you later."

"Ok Glen, see you later and good luck with your investigation."

Glen stopped by Ian's office on his way out.

"Ian, there is big trouble. There are nine people dead that either work here or have worked here. The common denominator is that all nine were on the list of lottery winners. Too much coincidence."

Ian replied, "I know that nothing can bring them back, and it's terrible that they are dead, but Glen, my company will be dead if I can't produce product. Please speed up your investigations so I can produce for my customers. Nothing can bring this company and its employees back from the dead. Too many employees involved here would be out of work."

"I hope I don't sound callous, but it's a reality. Ian, as long as no more dead bodies appear, the investigation should be concluded in about two days. We are zeroing in on a suspect."

Ian stared at Glen as if Glen would volunteer who it is that he is zeroing in on, but Glen volunteered nothing in the wake of this momentary silence.

"Here is your list, Glen. You need to scratch off the ones that will not be here to accept the checks. I didn't want to scratch them off in case you detectives had your own way of doing that."

"Thanks. Paige. That was considerate of you. I've got to go."

"What do you think of all these deaths, Paige?" asked Ian.

"It's incredible. I can't believe all these people are losing their lives. It's weird, especially since they were on the lottery list."

As Glen pulled out, his cell phone rang.

"Rita Wilson of the Lottery Corporation calling, sir. I called our local police station and they told me that you were investigating some deaths at Ianova Industries. We received a call from Ms. Paige Plane. She notified us that she and twenty-four others at Ianova Industries were in possession of the $275 million winning ticket. She scanned and e-mailed us the list with the names of the winners and the copy of the winning ticket. She later notified us that six names had been taken off the list. She notified us about three more today. Since lottery winnings are not paid if there is a police investigation, I felt it was best to phone and see what was happening since nine people out of twenty-five were taken off the list. That's a big amount to come off; we need to be sure whether there is a police investigation going on because Friday is when we are to come down to Ianova Industries with a news crew to present the winners with their checks."

"Yes, there is a police investigation going on, Rita. I am the detective heading it."

"Glad to know detective. I will need to hear from you when the investigation is concluded so we can resume the payout to the winners. Do you believe that there was foul play, sir?"

"I will call you when the investigation is over, but I cannot comment on the case except to say that there were suspicious deaths at Ianova Industries involving lottery winners."

"I will call Paige to let her know that this Friday's presentation is postponed until further notice."

"Thanks for the call, Rita."

"Take care, detective."

Rita called Paige right away.

"Paige, I just got off the phone with Glen Heron. He indicated that he is investigating some strange deaths at Ianova Industries where several winners lost their lives suspiciously. Therefore, per the guidelines put into position by the federal government and the

Lottery Corporation, there will be a delay in forwarding any winning funds until this investigation is closed."

Paige said, "I understand. I hope the killings stop because they are starting to scare me."

"They are starting to scare everyone. I will keep you informed."

"Okay," replied Paige. "Talk to you soon I hope. Good-bye."

RDE.TV pulled into Ianova Industries. Gail walked into the front office with her film crew.

She asked, "How do you feel about all nine murders, Vanity?"

Vanity replied, "What are you talking about? I know nothing about any murders? Who are you—and what are you doing here?"

Ian walked out to see what the commotion was.

He said, "Gail, get your people—and get out of here."

Gail said, "Why were nine people murdered? Isn't it a coincidence that all nine work here—or worked here? Isn't it a coincidence that all nine were on the winning lottery list? Isn't it also a coincidence that your son was on the list of winners, but he is still alive and well?"

"What do you mean? Are you saying he will die?"

"No. I'm saying he was the killer."

"You bitch," said Ian as he moved forward to punch Gail. She had a couple of heavyweights around her. "Get out of my building!" Ian was subdued by Gail's people.

"Don't like my pointed questions, Ian?" said Gail. "Don't forget you are being filmed. You almost assaulted me on film. Watch it."

"You're trespassing. Get out," said Ian.

"I hear your company is going bankrupt, Ian. I hear you need the money. Your son stands to get a lot of money—even more than budgeted if more people die. How do feel about that?"

"Get out of my building. You are trespassing and were not invited. Get off my property."

Barbara walked in. She looked at Gail and said, "My son said you were not invited. He told you to get out twice because you are trespassing. You are still here with your entourage. They are big men and scary looking with big muscles I feel very threatened by them. Oh, goodness. Why won't you leave? I feel like you are going to kill me. Oh my Goodness. I feel like I need to defend myself. I am feeling faint."

Barbara flipped her boiling coffee on Gail's face. Gail started screaming in pain. Barbara looked at the bodyguards and yelled, "Please don't kill me. Please don't kill me. I am an old lady. Please leave."

Gail's face was all red, and it looked like the skin would fall off.

Gail said, "Barbara, your grandson is a murderer. I know where he got his violence from."

Barbara said, "Vanity, call the police and tell them we have violent trespassers that are threatening me and my son and are not leaving my building."

"Don't worry, old lady," said Gail. "We are leaving."

"It's okay, Gail Slut. Oops, my mistake. I mean Gail Slut. Oops, there I go again naming you what everyone calls you behind your back. I meant Ms. Sclarz. I still want a police report because of your inappropriate behaviour."

Gail and her staff walked out. Gail was patting her face from the burning coffee.

"Thanks, Mom," said Ian.

"What are mothers for, son?"

Vanity said, "Mrs. Ianova, do you still want me to call the police?"

"Document all that happened here. Leave out the part where my son lunged at Gail to hit her. Insert that he calmly walked toward her instead. Send a copy by e-mail to Glen Heron, myself, and Ian."

"Okay, Mrs. Ianova. I will take care of that."

"Thanks dear," said Barbara. "I'm coming to your place for dinner tonight, Ian."

"Okay, Mom. That's great. I'm leaving. I'll see you there."

"Okay, I'm leaving in a few minutes as well. I'm going to shut my computer down."

Vanity started to type the report. She got into the details and typed what Barbara said to do about Ian. She hit the send button. The message arrived at Glen Heron's Blackberry.

Glen read it and was visibly upset by the message. He called Gail on her cell phone.

Glen said, "What the hell were you doing? Barbara wants to file trespassing charges against you and your staff and wants to charge you with threatening her."

"I have everything on video, Glen. It didn't happen like that. I'll show you the footage."

"I don't care about your footage. The video can never show what was on Barbara's mind. If she said she felt threatened, every court will believe the old lady. I have an investigation going on that is almost complete, and I don't need a reporter spoiling it."

"You mean you're going to arrest someone soon, Glen?"

"Yes. We are very close."

"I'll stay away, but I want to be the first to know when you will arrest someone."

"Okay. It's a deal. I have an update tonight on TV about this case, but no details—only vague news."

"Okay, Gail."

At Ianova Industries, everyone prepared to walk out as the day drew to a close. They were all getting ready to go home.

Ian walked into his office and read one last e-mail.

"Good night, Mr. Ianova."

"Good night, Vanity. See you in the morning."

The e-mail was from Vanity about what had happened in the office. He smiled as he read the part where he calmly walked up to Gail instead of lunging at her.

I guess that's what moms are for—protecting their young.

He shut down his laptop. He walked out and locked the door; he was the last to leave.

CHAPTER 12

More Bad News

Ian and Robert pulled into their home driveway and then walked in the front door.

Leah and Barbara were inside.

Leah said, "Come here, boys. Quick! There is some news about our company on TV."

All four of them are watching Gail's report with a distaste look on their faces.

"Shut it off I've seen enough of this crap," said Ian.

"Dad, what are these people talking about? They pretty much said that I killed all these people. Am I going to jail?"

"No. You're not. I'm calling Rod Brown, the nation's best criminal lawyer."

"Why?" asked Leah. "If you do that, everyone will think he is guilty."

"Robert has already been accused. They said everything except that Robert had been charged. I can see that happening anytime now the way this investigation is going."

"What's going to happen to me?"

"Nothing, son. Rod Brown will take care of this. I'll call him first thing in the morning."

They all make their way into the dining room where dinner is being served.

Ian looked at Leah and whispered so that Robert couldn't hear him and said, "I'm worried. Do you think Robert is capable of killing people in order to help me?"

"Oh my God. How can you think that way? What the heck do you think, that we raised—a monster?" Leah was almost yelling not caring that Robert could hear everything been said.

"Sorry, Leah. I can't think straight."

"Of course. Robert would not even entertain such a thing."

"No. He wouldn't. I can't believe what came out of your mouth. Don't ever talk like that to me again."

"Okay, honey. Sorry. I won't."

They all sat down to eat with no words being exchanged.

Robert got up before finishing his meal and said, "I'm going up to my room to relax. I'm not hungry anymore."

"But you hardly touched your meal," said Barbara.

"I'm not hungry," said Robert.

Up to his room he went.

Barbara said, "That poor kid. He must be going crazy inside after that news broadcast he heard. I'd be going crazy to if it were me. Imagine being accused of murdering your workmates."

"Wow. That is too much for anyone to handle."

"Make sure you call Rod Brown ASAP. The more I think about this, the more I can see the media groups around the world accusing Robert of murder."

"All the media wants is someone to blame—a scapegoat."

"That's right," said Barbara. "Glen and his deputies need someone to arrest; if they don't, the community won't feel like they were doing their jobs."

"They are all crazy."

Ian's cell phone is ringing. It is Tony Neil calling.

"Good evening Tony"

"Good evening to you Ian."

"I'm surprised your still in your office Tony".

"Don't forget Ian, I have 3 hours on you, I am on the west coast".

"Ah yes of course, that's right. How can I help you?"

"Ian, I heard about what is happening to your company. I have no option here, I am canceling my deal with Ianova Industries."

"You can't do that!"

"I can—and I am. I discussed it with my attorneys before I called you. I am totally within my right to cancel the deal based on what is going on with your company."

"Tony, that will kill me. Our deal is integral to my emergence from Chapter 11."

"Sorry. Ian. In fact the projects you are working on for me currently, need to be sped up. You need to increase production—and I have no option, I need to hold back monies until they are complete."

Ian said, "How can I buy materials to produce for you if you won't pay me?"

"Simple. Send me your material charges from your suppliers, and I will pay them directly. You can still deliver for me, and my interests are protected. You can still make your money. However, any new projects are dead until you prove to the courts that you are a viable company."

"Tony, I can't believe you are doing this to me."

"Ian, why not stop blaming others for your company's demise and start asking how you can do this to your customers? Your customers are not to blame—you are!"

"Okay, Tony. Your mind is made up. I can sense that. Thanks for the call, and we'll speak to you shortly after I emerge from bankruptcy protection."

"There you go, Ian," that's the spirit. We'll talk to you soon, my friend—and good luck!"

Barbara can see that Ian is very upset after the phone call with Tony and says to Ian, "It will all work out, you will see."

"It had better work out, I am going to bed now," said Ian. Ian walked out.

Leah said, "Barbara, is the company really in that bad shape?"

Barbara said, "It is in really bad shape. I will be very surprised if it emerges at all from Chapter 11—even though I am very hopeful that it does. Ian is a great son, a great father, and a great husband, but as a businessman, he is too nice. He needs to be more firm at the production part of the company and he really needs to give crap to people that deserve it. He needs to fire people that deserve it instead of hoping that things work themselves out. Things don't work themselves out by themselves, Leah. People know what they can get away with and what they can't get away with. Everyone at Ianova Industries knows that. That's why I brought my people on board to remedy that situation. Unfortunately I wonder if it's too late."

"I sure hope it's not too late," replied Leah. "Will you put some of your own money back into the company?"

"Good night, dear," said Barbara. Without answering Leah's question.

"Good night," said Leah.

* * *

A jet was beginning to come in for a landing at a small airport in Arizona. The pilot claimed he had lost control of the aircraft due to hydraulic pressure loss. The flight had been uneventful right from takeoff, but the controls had been getting sluggish as the pilots prepared for descent.

The right and left turns were delayed. The up and down aeons were also working but also sluggish and hard to move. The hydraulics were not working. Alarms were going off in the cockpit, indicating no hydraulic pressure. The pilots were doing what they could, but without hydraulic pressure in the lines, they couldn't turn or control the elevation of the aircraft. The fight seemed hopeless and becomes apparent that they have a critical situation.

"Mayday! We have no control—all hydraulic pressure is gone. I only can power engines on the left and right to try to create a turn. I have no elevation controls other than accelerating for altitude and slowing down for approach."

"Use runway two left for final approach, and we will send fire rescue to that section. Slow down—you're coming in too fast."

"Can't slow down. I have no flaps. I'm going to touch down and slam the breaks."

"You won't have the runway room. Accelerate and try to go around again."

"I believe I have only one shot at this" The pilot quickly says to the passengers through the speaker system, "Fasten your seatbelts and brace for impact."

"Accelerate full throttle. You're too low. You won't make it. Accelerate. Accelerate."

"Oh God. I am accelerating."

As the pilot accelerated, he was climbing too slowly to clear the desert mountain in front of him. He couldn't angle his flaps to get maximum lift because of the lack of hydraulic pressure.

"We are going to hit, we're going to hit, we're going to hit" screamed the pilot. "God help us!"

"Oh my Goodness. Search and rescue, follow the fire on the mountain and get me survivors."

"We see it," replied search and rescue. "We are on our way."

Search and rescue arrived at the scene and searched through debris only to find wreckage in millions of small pieces and no survivors. Little clumps of fire surround the crash site. The report went back to the flight's origin through the control tower and found the origin was in Toronto. The manifest was ordered to find out how many passengers were on board. It was determined that twelve passengers, a pilot, a co-pilot, and one crew member were on board. All fifteen souls on board perished.

Night fell and search and rescue confirmed the terrible news that there were no survivors. The control tower put out an order for runway two to be closed until investigators could see whether there was any sign of hydraulic fluid.

In the morning, investigators found a section of fuselage that had controls on it. One section was the hydraulic area that had valves on it. It was interesting to see that it had a switch that was turned into the "drain" position that allowed hydraulic fluids to be drained during maintenance procedures.

Police detectives at the plane crash scene asked the FAA investigators if that switch could have shifted from the lock position to the drain position during the impact. The FAA said no because the switch was protected by a safety case that needed to be removed first in order to gain access to the switch.

The investigator showed the detective the assembly portion that still had the safety case surrounding the switch. The case had to be in the locked position prior to take off or alarms would sound in the cockpit. The pilots would not have taken off with an alarm sounding. They would have called maintenance to fix the problem. The switch was in the "drain" position.

The detective looked at the FAA investigator and asked what he thought.

The FAA investigator replied, "Someone wanted this plane down for insurance claims or wanted the passengers dead."

"How can you be so sure?"

"You cannot close and lock this case with the switch in the drain position. As you close the case, this action forces the switch to the nondrain position automatically in case you forget to manually move it. The only other way it would close and remain in the drain position is if you trip or break the mechanism that automatically moves the switch to nondrain when closing the case. You can see here that the mechanism—in this case, a mechanical mechanism—was missing. That means whoever closed this case, broke the mechanical mechanism on purpose so that the switch could be left in the drain position and the case could be locked, and no alarms would sound in the cockpit. The plane was doomed from takeoff—and no one would know until hydraulics leaked out and then were needed in order to activate the controls."

"Could the mechanic in Toronto in charge of maintenance on this aircraft have broken the mechanical mechanism and not had known it?"

"No way. The mechanism is a built-in feature from the factory. It was enclosed. A human can't touch it or get at it. Someone who knew what they were doing had to come in here with a very sharp and strong object and had to slowly chisel the mechanism away. Whoever did the last maintenance on this aircraft had to sign off on it. There would be murder charges against him if this plane went down because he would be responsible. The easy way to check is to see if whoever signed off on this aircraft is still working today. If he is still working, he probably is innocent. If his whereabouts are unknown, he is probably responsible for the crash."

"We'll leave that up to Toronto's end of the investigation."

The Toronto police chief was contacted with the news. He sent the information to Glen Heron.

CHAPTER 13

The Arrest

Leah, Ian and Robert were in the kitchen. They were tired because none of them had gotten a normal night's sleep.

Ian said, "I wonder what surprises today will bring."

Leah said, "It will be a good day today." She was all smiles because she knew how worried Robert was. "We will hear great news today."

Robert said, "I feel like puking. I have a really bad feeling about today. Glen Heron thinks I'm totally guilty and he wants to arrest me ASAP and throw me in jail. I don't want to go to work today."

Barbara walked in and said, "Don't worry, Robert. Grandma won't let anything happen to you." She hugged Robert and Robert hugged her tight.

Ian looked at Leah with a very worried look on his face. He knew it was a real possibility that Robert would be arrested. Detective Glen Heron needs a arrest badly.

"I'm off," said Ian.

"Good day, honey," said Leah as she walked over to Ian. "Robert and your mom are still hugging. Wow, it's like their last hug. Please call the lawyer right away. I think we'll need him."

"I know," replied Ian.

"See you later, Dad."

"Okay, Robert, but make it fast because it won't look good if you are late."

"I'll be right behind you, Dad."

As Ian drove toward his office, he heard a radio broadcast.

Jesse Meeler said, "Ianova Industries will have more turbulence coming their way this morning. We have acquired a report that indicates a jetliner went down in Arizona with twelve Ianova Industries employees last night. Not one survivor was found. The report suggests that the mission has changed from search and rescue to search and recover. More on Ian Ianova is our Mary Denim. Hi Mary"

"Hi Jesse"

"Mary, is there anything you can tell us about the plane crash in Arizona or about Mr. Ianova?"

"Yes I can Jesses about Ian but not about the plane crash, this is really tough for Mr. Ianova. He is quite the leader in his community with all the services he has provided all these years, he has touched the hearts of so many people with his generosity. The hype of car accidents, lottery winnings, lottery killings, bankruptcy and so on, it makes you wonder how much of this Ian and his family can withstand before they break down. Mr. Ianova, if you are listening out there, we are with you. We know that you will come out of this scandal clean. He also employs about 1,400 local people. He is a leader in this community. Mr. Ianova, our prayers are with you."

Ian couldn't believe what he heard about more employees dying—twelve of them. He smacked his steering wheel and swore out loud. He got to his office before anyone else. He unlocked the door and went straight to his office. He knew that Gail of RDE.TV would broadcast the news about the jetliner accident anytime now and put her own spin on the way she broadcasts because she had been right on top of the investigation. Ian got into his paperwork and looked through his directory for Rod Brown's cell phone number. It was 7:30; he knew it was too early to call Rod.

Ian looked at a picture in his office wondering if Robert really was killing people to help him out.

The news broadcast begins as Ian has his TV turned on, Gail Sclarz is speaking but Ian is not really listening. Gail says in summary some of what other news broadcasters and the viewers have been saying, "It will all come out in the wash. What was really happening here?" Another said, "Where there is smoke, there is fire. Someone at Ianova Industries is killing—regardless of how clean that company looked on the outside." Another said, "Ian Ianova is another rich person taking advantage of whatever he can, thinking he is invincible and can't be touched—whether regarding him or his family. Another said, "I love Ian and his family. He has helped this community with time and money when he never had to do a thing. There you have it folks said Gail. You hear what the viewers and news broadcasters are saying about this case. However, nothing will prepare you for what I am going to tell you next. Listen to this.

Tony Tuscony, Blair Hinder, Tim Timberlake, Josh Kaychuch, Julie Grey, Carrie Turner, Janet Brooke, Vito Vitorrio, Nick De La Rokos, Ellen Wolf, Dana Carriage, Teneal Taylor all lost their lives last night in a plane crash. And not only were all the passengers employees at Ianova Industries, they were all on the list of lottery winners. These twelve people chartered a small jet to tour the Grand Canyon before returning to work for what may have been their last week of work before a wealthy retirement. They booked this trip on their Visa cards, hoping to pay their trip off with their lottery winnings this Friday. That will never happen now. They will rest in peace—but not in the manner that they thought. The speculation of who is killing everyone is growing. That speculation is pointing to someone at Ianova Industries."

Ian shut off the TV and called Rod Brown's cell regardless of the fact that it is still early.

"Good morning this is Rod Brown speaking"

Good morning Rod this is Ian speaking. I'll get right to it Rod. I know you heard what is going on here, can you help us?"

"If you are innocent, I will."

"I am for sure. However, speculation about my son is running at a million miles per hour."

"You mean $275 million miles per hour?"

"That's not funny, Rod, however very accurate."

"Do you hear me laughing, Ian? Don't you think that is what the world is thinking? The police need to arrest someone. The public needs to think the police are doing their jobs or all chaos will break loose because there are too many people dying. Your son will be arrested this morning."

Ian swallowed as he heard Rod talking. "Can you come to my office this morning?

"I sure will. Do you know where we are located?"

"Everyone knows where you are located. I'll be there in three hours. I'll have to let my girls know what is happening and let my colleagues handle my appointments for next few days since you will need me badly."

"I'll see you in a few hours."

Leah, Barbara and Robert all walked in together. The streets were lined with news media and reporters. Security officers patrolling Ian's building were in front of the building holding the crowd back so employees could get in. Robert had a worried look on his face as he saw all the people.

Barbara said, "Goodness, they have convicted us without a day in court."

As they walked from the car to the office, the media was yelling at them.

"Robert, how did it feel to kill innocent people for your father's gain? Murderer, die in hell."

Robert went into his office to try to hide his feelings. Robert and Leah started to weep as they feared the worst might be happening.

Back at the police station, Glen and his detectives also were watching the news broadcast. The Arizona police had confirmed that someone in Toronto tampered with the hydraulic switch and wanted the plane to crash. After Glen had received the names of souls onboard, he compared them to the lottery list. *Robert, what the heck have you done?*

Glen needed three pieces of vital information to come back to him with results before he could decide what action to take on the first nine killings. Was the color on the bumper of the F-150 the same as the color of the car that went over the cliff? What vehicle did the tread belong to from the scene of the F-150 discovery? Could he place Robert Ianova without a doubt behind the wheel? The three results were due within the hour—and were critical to an arrest being made.

Back at the office, Ian listened to his messages.

Pierce said, "Ian, you are so full of lies, it is incredible. You're not going bankrupt? Behind our backs, you send letters that you are going bankrupt. You're a lying SOB! I guess I do have to sue you so I can get some funds out of you."

Leval said, "Ian, I know times are tough for you, but you're making your problem my problem. Pay out of your personal funds. I need something or I'm closing my doors. Are you going to let that happen to me because of you?"

Ian put his head down and started pulling his hair.

"Ian, this is Ron Branson. I have not seen any action on my project. You said you would send in your forces immediately to take care of your problem. I have no option but to call in your insurance company that holds your labor, performance, and material bonds. Also, I have no option but to hold back your 15 percent construction fee and finish this work myself. I can't believe you are letting me down. You have let this slip to the point where you are costing me a grand opening. Also Ian, buddy, what the heck is happening up there? The news we are hearing is not good. When you are back on the saddle and on top of things, call me."

Ian put his head down and screamed, "What is going on here? Why me?"

Spiro said, "Ian, when will you stop your lies and pay us? I guess we need to hire our own lawyer and come in with a class action lawsuit against you like we said. Oh well, you started this."

Frank said, "Ian, come on. This is my third message. Why the heck are you hiding, you coward? Talk to me."

Ian had heard enough—even though there were eight more messages.

Back at the police station, an officer explained the report as soon as it came in. The paint on the front end of the F-150 was the same paint from the car that went over the cliff. The tread mark results show that it was from a 2012 Cadillac Escalade. Escalades started using a new brand of tire in 2012. No other vehicle was using them. Robert drove a Cadillac Escalade, but they could not put him behind the wheel of the F-150. Whoever drove the F-150 was smart enough to wipe everything down. There were no prints anywhere. The team went over it three times, but the vehicle was clean.

"I don't care," said Glen. "It's close enough. He did it! Let's get him on these murder charges locally—and then we can charge him later for the twelve on the aircraft."

"You mean fifteen on the aircraft, sir. There were three crew members."

"If there were twenty-five people on the winning list, a total of twenty-one people on the list have died. Shouldn't we have twenty-four-hour guards on the other four?"

"We are going to arrest the murderer. The killings will stop. Besides, Robert would probably want to share the winnings with the three remaining people so it looks like he didn't kill everyone. What an amateur way of thinking."

Rod Brown pulled into Ianova Industries and introduced himself to reception.

Vanity said, "Mr. Ianova is expecting you. His office is the first one on your right."

"Great to meet you, Ian." Robert was paged to go into his dad's office. "All I have heard about you and your firm has been great—except the last week. You're in deep, Ian."

"I know. That's why you are here to prove our innocence." Robert walked in. "Robert, this is Rod Brown. Rod, this is my son."

With sirens blaring, at least ten cars were en route to Ianova Industries to arrest Robert. Glen got out of his car and Gail ran toward him.

"Glen, you promised me that you would keep me informed. What are you doing here? Are you going to arrest Ian?"

"You'll get your story, Gail. Get yourself and your people back." Glen walked into the reception area and yelled, "Where is Robert?"

Rod Brown walked out and said, "I am the attorney representing the Ianova family. What do you want?"

Glen said, "I wonder why the Ianova family has hired the best criminal lawyer in the industry."

"Thanks for the flattery, Mr. Heron. What do you want?"

"I have a warrant for Robert Ianova's arrest for the first degree murder of nine people."

"You better have your ducks in a row because I will squash you and your investigation like a mashed potato."

"Oh I do. Believe me—the fifteen people in the Arizona plane crash will also be linked to Robert." Robert came out of his dad's office with Ian. "You are under arrest for the deaths of Peter Bixby, Bill Bixby, Liz Dunslap, Margo Sanchez, Sam Gunner, Paul Lazarus, Chris Phelentino, John Grey, and Phil Epson."

"Dad," yelled Robert.

"Arrest him," said Glen.

Barbara and Leah saw the handcuffs coming from one officer.

"You have a right to an attorney."

"Mom, Grandma, help me. You said this would not happen."

Barbara lunged toward the deputy who was about to cuff Robert.

Glen said, "Don't. You'll be charged for hindering an investigation."

"Arrest me, but let the boy go."

"If you cannot afford an attorney—"

Rod said, "We are aware of our rights."

"Take him away."

"Don't let them take me!"

Robert was escorted out of the building. The media crew took photos and asked questions, but the police didn't answer a single question. They made their way to the police station for the booking process and a court date to set bond. As the police cruiser pulled out, objects were thrown at the car and the yelling was incredible.

"Murderer! Die in hell!"

Leah and Barbara cried in the reception area. Rod indicated that bond would be set in a few days. When the family posted bail, Robert would be out of prison until a trial date was set.

Ian quietly backed away and went into his office. He sat in his chair, stared at the family picture, and started weeping. He could not believe what was happening.

CHAPTER 14

It's Not Over

Leval Preston, Adam Wendell, Ventres Hullman, Pierce Tredline, Spiro Meeles, and Frank Ianaetti all just walked in unannounced to Ianova Industries.

Vanity said, "I will be right there, gentlemen. I am making another pot of coffee."

"Go ahead, Vanity. We can wait."

Vanity sticks her head into Ian's office and says, "I have six gentlemen—all your suppliers—standing at reception, demanding a meeting with you, sir." "Barbara looks at Ian and says, see them, Ian. We will step out. Tell them the truth. We have no money—let them sue. We'll close the doors and start over. Remember, they can't touch us personally. Whatever we have now—we'll have forever. It's more than enough for the rest of our lives."

Paige walks into the reception area and they all say hello as they all know each other. The coffee pot is ready, Vanity and Paige and all the men are in the reception area drinking coffee and talking. They laugh they joke and Adam Wendell and Paige Plane are off to the side a little on their own talking. Paige seems very upset about their conversation, in fact she is wiping tears away from her face. Mr. Ianova, calls Vanity.

"Okay. Send them in, Vanity,"

The six men walked into Ian's office.

Ian said, "There is no way to sugar coat this so I will just say it. I have no money. I lost my largest account that was going to get me out of this mess. I may have to close my doors and reopen."

"You are going to screw us," said Pierce, president of Woodboard Industries.

"Listen, guys. You have all been with me for years. Please bear with me. I will repay each of you, weather it's tomorrow, next month, or next year. I promise you that."

"Screw you, Ian," said Pierce. "We have heard nothing but lies from you."

The men got up, made their way to their cars, and drove away.

* * *

Robert was being booked at the police station.

Glen looked at Robert and asked, "Did you really think that you would get away with killing all these people?"

"I killed no one!"

"All the evidence points to you, Robert. We can place you at each murder site."

"Then you have done something wrong—and you will never be able to prove anything. I want my parents and my lawyer."

"I don't think they—or anyone else—can help you this time."

* * *

Ian's limo driver, Rex Hill, was on call. He turned up the music on his alarm. It was 10:30am. *Wow. I've got it good. I get to sleep in, and I won't get in crap for it.* Ian only used him for meetings during the day. Rex went into the bathroom to get ready. He shaved and then stepped into the shower.

Rex stepped out of the shower and started to dry himself off. He sang to himself a little bit and started dancing a bit. His towel limited his movement. He got out the hair dryer and started drying his hair. He went to the kitchen and started filling a coffee pot with water. He sniffed a weird smell, but he continued to fill the pot. He put the full pot on the gas stove burner and turned the knob. He heard the click of the ignition and then a boom! His house blew up. A neighbour called 911.

* * *

Police dispatch calls Detective Glen Heron and lets him know about the gas explosion. Glen writes down the address and repeats it to the dispatch so as to be sure he wrote it down correctly.

"Ok it's 1067B Wilkinson Ave. Got it thanks, bye now."

"Hey, I know that address"

"What are you talking about, Robert? You know the guy who owns the home at 1067B Wilkinson?"

"Absolutely I do."

"How do you know him?"

"He works for my dad's company."

"What a coincidence that is. Was Rex Hill one of the lottery winners?"

Robert said, "Yes."

"I already knew the answer to that question. I did not have to ask you."

"Glen, if I am in here being arrested for all these lottery pool deaths, how could I have possibly blown up Rex's house?"

"You could have planted or done something last night on a timer or something. Who knows how a lunatic like you thinks. Robert, you can be sure of one thing—I will prove whatever I need to prove, and you will be charged with all counts of first-degree murder for everyone that has died."

Robert pulled back five or six paces and whispered, "You got the wrong guy."

"What did you say, Robert?"

"I said nothing."

Glen walked out of the police station and started to make his way to his car. He started his journey to Rex Hill's home to see what the heck was going on.

As he started driving, Glen started to calculate. *With Rex being dead, there are three lottery winners left. Robert is alive and well. Paige Plane is alive and well. Who is the third person? I better put protection on whoever that is.*

Glen radioed into dispatch.

"Who is the remaining lottery winner—other than Robert Ianova and Paige Plane? Check the list and let me know as soon as possible because we may need twenty-four-hour security around them."

"Will do, sir."

Glen got very frustrated because of how many murders there had been. *Could Robert orchestrate this stuff? He seems kind of goofy to scheme these murders up.* Glen started punching the steering wheel in anger. He was in front of Rex Hill's burnt home. It was smoldering because the firefighters had extinguished the flames already. He got out of his car and started walking toward the burnt home. He saw the fire chief and started walking toward him.

"What do we have here?" asked Glen.

The chief said, "We pulled out the occupant of the home. White male, about six feet tall. He was unconscious when we got here—probably from the explosion. Judging by what we see here, this was a classic case of someone not turning off the gas valve of the stove completely. The kitchen area filled up with gas from the constant leak overnight and then, when turning on the stove in the morning, you get a big boom."

Glen asked, "Isn't there an auto shut off on the stove so gas does not leak."

"Yes, there is on new stoves—but not on old products."

"Don't you think that the occupant could have smelled the gas as he walked into the kitchen?"

The chief said, "Maybe and maybe not. The gas is a little heavier than air, so it may have been under the occupant's nose level. He may have missed the smell. The guy was just waking up. Even if he did smell something, he may have dismissed it."

"Do you think that someone could have come in last night or early this morning and turned the knob to bypass the ignition?"

"Of course they could have, but why would you ask that question?"

"Thinking of all angles. One last question—what time would you say the explosion happened?"

"The 911 call came in this morning at 10:50 from a neighbour. The explosion probably happened five minutes or so before that."

"Okay. Thanks." Glen turned and walked away.

Paige Plane looked around her to see if anyone was watching and turned her computer to the news channel. She watched Gail

Sclarz broadcast the explosion at Rex's house. She paged Vanity and asked if Rex was on the lottery list.

"Yes. He was."

"Ok, so Robert was in prison. You were here. Who was the last person on the list? There are three of you left with Rex dead."

Paige said, "Wow, I never thought of that. It is Leah Ianova! She is the last person on the list"

"I bet you that she was the one that killed everyone so that the Ianova's get the winnings."

"I will call Detective Heron and tell him that I need protection."

Ian watched Leah, his mother, and Rod walk into his office.

Leah said, "How did it go, honey?"

Ian said, "How do you think it went? It sucked—that's how it went."

Rod said, "I will go work on posting bail for Robert.

"Thanks, Rod," said Ian, Leah, and Barbara almost in unison.

"Leah, Mom, let's go for lunch"

As they walked past reception, Ian said they were all going out for lunch. Leah looked through the side of her eye at Vanity. Vanity shivered as she looked back in fear, thinking that Leah was the mass murderer.

A call came in from dispatch to Glen.

"Sir, we have located Leo Chuckhill, the mechanic for the airliner that went down in Arizona."

"Where is he?"

"He is at work, sir. He reported to work."

"Okay," said Glen. "Get me a warrant. I want to go search everything where he works. What part of the airport did he work in?"

"He works in the VIP hangar. Consider the warrant done, sir."

CHAPTER 15

A New Day

Glen started his day by showering, shaving, and then getting a coffee at the local drive through. He was en route to the police station to pick up the search warrant so he and his investigating team could look for evidence at Leo Chuckhill's place of work. He walked into the police station, gathered his team, and made his way to the airport.

He walked out of his car with his team behind him and said, "I am looking for Leo Chuckhill."

A mechanic pointed to an office. Glen walked into Leo's office and introduced himself as the detective in charge of the plane crash investigation.

"Were you the one that signed off on the plane's maintenance?"

Leo said, "Yes."

"How do you sign off on something that was not airworthy?"

Leo stands up in a defensive appearance as people generally are proud of their work and responds,

"Sir, when I signed off on that plane, it was airworthy. It was in perfect mechanical condition, and nothing was wrong with it."

"Then why did it crash?"

"I don't know why it crashed. We tested the hydraulic pressure. There were no leaks. There were no holes. The pressure was perfect. We stressed the pressure lines, and they were perfect. There was nothing wrong with that aircraft. I heard the news media, they say that the hydraulic pressure loss was the cause of the crash. I'm telling you that the aircraft was in perfect running order when it left here"

"You realize that if we find that you were negligent, you can be held accountable for the deaths of all the persons on board."

"You don't have to worry about that, sir. If I was negligent, I would not burden the system by going into prison. I will take my own life because I do not deserve to live. I would deserve to be with the souls onboard."

"Some people look forward to that thinking they are going to a better place, Leo. Are you one of those people?"

"No. I am not!"

Glen twirled his finger in the air to tell his investigating team to start looking around.

"What do you suspect happened Leo?"

"I suspect Glen that someone came in here after we all left to go home and tampered with the plane."

"How did someone gain access to do what was required? It is a tedious job—and what clearance is required to come in here?"

"The security clearance is at the gate. You have to clear security when driving in. Once you're in, you have pick of the litter to do whatever you want."

Glen's cell phone rang.

"It's dispatch, sir. The last name on the lottery list is Leah Ianova."

Glen hung up the phone and was visibly shocked. He said, "Get me a list of everyone who went through security the night prior to the crash. Leo, was anyone allowed through the security gate?"

"No, sir. It's only for people who own aircraft here, their friends in the same vehicle, and wealthy people who have chartered aircraft. They need to have a boarding pass and a passport with them for regular screening."

"Thanks for all your help." Glen looked at his investigating team. "Report back to me with anything you find."

Glen got into his car and started driving to Ianova Industries. *Robert was plain stupid to think of all those murders and sabotaging the plane, but Leah has been around private planes most of her life. She would know what to do to cause a hydraulic leak. Paige was an innocent bystander. Was it a tag team between mom and son? Well, let's find out Leah.*

Glen pulls into Ianova Industries and at reception he asks to speak to Leah. Vanity pages Leah and lets her know that Glen wants to see her, and Leah responds to Vanity to let Glen into Ian's office in 5 minutes. Vanity says ok. Leah went into Ian's office and told Ian that Glen was here to see her. She didn't want to talk to Glen alone.

Ian said, "Yes, of course. No worries, but what the heck does he want? He already has our son in jail? Leah does he want you in jail to?"

Glen walks into Ian's office and says, "Good morning."

"What is good about it?" asked Ian. "You have my son in your jail."

"You have a great lawyer. I'm sure Robert will be out today by noon."

"You're missing the point, Glen. What do you want?"

"I want to congratulate Leah on her winnings."

"What are you talking about?" asked Leah.

Glen said, "You are on the list of winners! You, Robert, and Paige are the three left. That's $275 million divided by three people—over $91 million each. Not a bad payday."

"Wow," said Leah. "That is a big payday. I guess we will be okay after all."

Glen said, "You seemed to be unaware that you were on the list."

"I am surprised. My son and I talked about putting me on the list. It was my first time in the pool—and we won. Yes, it is surprising to me because I forgot all about it."

"Forgot all about it? $275 million and your husband's company going bankrupt and you forgot all about it? Twenty-two murders and you forgot all about it? How about you, Ian? Do you buy tickets?"

Ian opened his top drawer, pulled out five hundred tickets, and said, "These are all non winning tickets that I bought. I'll sell them all to you for a dollar."

"No thanks."

Ian looked at Glen and said, "You have known my family for years. We are friends. You know deep inside—regardless of how the evidence looks—nobody in my family had anything to do with the murders."

Glen said, "My training tells me to let the evidence do the speaking—the truth will come out."

Ian said, "When I went to law school—yes, that's right, I went to law school before you did—my training said to seek new evidence until you are satisfied inside." Ian pounded his chest with one arm. "You haven't done that yet, Glen, because you arrested my son. That did not make sense because he did nothing wrong—and he was innocent."

Glen got up to leave and looked back at Ian and at Leah. "Maybe when this is all over, we will look back in shock and in disbelief if Robert was not responsible for the murders. God help us."

Glen walked out to his car and received a phone call.

"Detective Glen Heron Speaking"

"This is Rita Wilson from lottery corporation sir, good morning"

"Good morning Rita, how can I help you?"

"I just wanted to get updated on the Ianova Industry case sir because Paige from Ianova Industries called and said to take one additional person, a—Rex Hill—off of the list. That only leaves Robert Ianova, Leah Ianova, and Paige Plain on the list"

Glen asks "When did Paige phone you this morning with the update about Rex? It sure seems kind of hurried that she would phone that fast so soon after the explosion."

"This morning? Oh no sir, she phoned yesterday morning."

"What did you just say Rita?"

"It was yesterday morning that she phoned sir. She said there was a gas explosion and that Rex was in the house and died from the blast."

"What time did she call?"

"The time she phoned, one moment sir, I have it right here bear with me, yes here it is, it was at 10:30am, sir."

Glen's head was buzzing; he turned his body in a circle, almost falling down in disbelief.

"Rita, how sure are you about the time she phoned?"

"It was a recorded call, because of the amount of money involved, the time of 10:30 and in fact 14 seconds is a 100% accurate time."

"You mean you only recorded Ianova Industry calls because of the big amount of money?"

"No sir we record all calls because all money is big to the winners."

"Thanks for your help, Rita. I will be in touch shortly."

"Ok Detective, have a great day sir"

Glen got in his car and started to drive away. He passes Paige's window and sees her talking on the telephone with a big smile. *I guess you are the one that can shock us all about the murders.* Glen now dials to call the fire chief and leaves a voicemail as the phone is not answered. Paige looks out the window and sees Glen staring at her. She waves and smiles. Glen smiles back, waves, and drives off. *My God, could Paige have done all these things?*

What time did you call yesterday Paige? Hum, 10:30 according to Rita. What time did the fire chief say the explosion happened?

Glen sort of envisions the fire chief telling him the time of the explosion but his vision fogs out when the part about the time approaches. He shakes his head in disbelief. He keeps driving through traffic and keeps thinking.

Glen's cell phone rings.

"Glen speaking."

"Arnold Boyer calling, the fire chief. I am returning your call."

"I hope your memory is better than mine, I know that you gave me the tentative time that you think that the explosion at Rex Hill's home happened. I am hoping that you can give me that time again."

"I sure can, Glen. However, the only thing is you mentioned tentative time—we have an exact time of explosion: 10:43am."

"How can you have an exact time?"

"There was a camera at an intersection less than two blocks away. The blast force moved the camera ever so slightly, but the convincing evidence was the bright light from the blast itself. It told the story—and it told the time."

"Why wasn't I informed of this Arnold?"

"Glen, we concluded our investigation of the blast about an hour ago. The video is being couriered to your office along with our investigation report showing the details. I think we did pretty good to conclude this investigation so fast."

"Okay. I will review it. How can you see a bright light from the blast if the blast happened in daylight?"

Arnold said, "It was unmistakable. You have to see it yourself."

"I will anxiously await it."

Glen pulled into his parking space and started to walk into the building. He passed a bunch of people who were looking at him strangely. Sergeant Hans Prague and Detective Stan Hady followed Glen into his office.

Glen asked, "What is going on? Why are you following me?"

Stan said, "Robert Ianova made bail. Rod Brown got him out."

"We couldn't hold him any longer."

"Big deal—let him go Stan."

"Why the easygoing attitude? We have further evidence that proves Robert killed the Bixby brothers—and potentially sabotaged the aircraft in Arizona."

"What is the evidence Stan? I bet it is nothing more than circumstantial."

"We found little metal and plastic filings on the ground at the airport. They were the filings from someone chiseling away at the safety clips of the housing that held the drain switch of the hydraulics in position. We also have an eyewitness who placed Robert one block away from the Bixby crash scene in a new Cadillac Escalade."

"Is there anyone who can place Robert or has evidence of Robert at the airport?"

"No" replies Stan and Hans at the same time.

Glen said, "I think this is nothing more than a goose chase. Robert didn't kill these people. Robert is too dumb for this kind of stuff. Yes, Robert does have knowledge of aircraft he has grown up around them all his life, flying them, illegally, cause he has no pilot's license in fact Robert has never taken a flying lesson in his life, he has cleaned them, been in them, but technical stuff? No way. He doesn't know how to change batteries on a electric knife."

"So if not Robert, who did it then?" asks Stan.

"I have my theories, but I need one more piece of the puzzle before I can tell you who it is."

"What piece?"

"It is a video that should arrive in a few minutes."

Glen told dispatch that he was expecting a parcel from the fire chief. When it came, it had to be delivered to his office immediately.

Dispatch said that the parcel had arrived and that it would be sent up ASAP.

"Great," said Glen. "Okay, boys. After reviewing the video, I hope we will have our murderer."

CHAPTER 16

New Evidence, New Arrest

The video came into Glen's office; he anxiously signed for it and began to open it. He stuck it into the CD player. They sat back and waited for the video to begin.

The intersection that was pictured in the video was in North Toronto, which was around the same intersection where Rex lives. And sure enough, there was a flash on the video and a small shaking of the camera itself from the blast wave at 10:43AM.

Glen said, "What do you think, boys?"

Stan said, "We know the blast happened. This was nothing new. What else should we gather from this?"

Hans said, "Before we do anything, why not go back and rewind. Let's see if any cars drove by earlier."

Glen said, "Great idea. At about two o'clock in the morning, a Cadillac Escalade came out of the parking lot where Rex lives."

"Look at that," said Stan. "Isn't that Ian's Cadillac that Robert was driving?"

Glen said, "It must be, but that makes no sense."

"Zoom in on the face," said Hans.

Glen zoomed in, but they could not make out the image.

Glen said, "Something is wrong here. Hand me the Bixby file, Stan. It's right beside you."

Stan handed Glen the file, and he started to flip through the pages.

"There it is!"

"What is it Glen?"

"Robert was driving a black Cadillac Escalade. This video shows a white Escalade."

"That is still weird," said Hans.

"Why?"

"Because nobody would be in this neighbourhood if they could afford an Escalade."

I agree, but surely you would have a visitor who drove one."

"I don't know about that. You know the old saying: show me your friends and I will tell you who you are. A rich person generally hangs with their own kind—not with people without money." Says Hans.

"So what are you saying?"

"I really don't know what I am saying—other than I believe this Cadillac was involved in one way or another because it was not in that neighbourhood just passing through at 2am. I just don't know how it is involved, but it is."

"Fair enough," said Glen. Stan, take this video to the lab. See if they can clear up the grain and get us an ID on the driver."

Stan said, "Okay. Will do." He left Glen's office.

"Ok, here is what I have Hans. Sit down. Paige Plane, you know who I mean?"

"Yes I do, she is the person in charge of the lottery pool at Ianova Industries."

"Yes that's correct Hans. Anyways, what she has done is she called a Rita Wilson at Lottery Corporation to update Rita about the murders that have been happening because all of the murders, 100% of them as you know are people that are on the winning lottery"

"Yes. So far that seems very normal because she needs to do that so Rita knew who to make the checks payable to."

"Yes, but here is the kicker. The last murder was at 10:43 when Rex's house blew up. At 10:30, Rita got a call from Paige telling her that Rex had died and that Rex's name had to come off the list. That was a full thirteen minutes before the blast. Rita asked Paige what had happened to Rex. Paige's answer was that he died in a gas leak explosion in his house. How would Paige know that this had happened when it didn't even happen yet?"

Hans said, "Holy crap! I can't believe this, but I guess money is the root of all evil. She is the murderer, Glen. The evidence speaks for itself—and you know what else? She was taking flying lessons and had been doing so for about one year. Part of flying lessons is knowing how the aircraft operates. I am sure that Paige broke the mechanism on the crashed plane as well. Has the list come back of all persons entering the airport security?"

Glen said, "Wow. I didn't know she was taking flying lessons. The list is right here, but I haven't looked at it yet."

He picked up the list and said, "Okay, let's see. Here it is. It was Paige. She did come into the airport the night before the flight took off."

Hans looked at Glen in disbelief and said, "Paige is the murderer? I don't believe it."

Glen said, "If you think about it, she worked for Ian for fifteen years. In that time, she walked through the plant, watched saw blades being changed, and watched how things were stacked and stored. She had gained enough knowledge over time to know and understand how things get done."

"That makes sense," said Hans.

"How did you know she had taken flying lessons?"

"I heard her joke to the people going to Arizona that she should pilot the plane but couldn't because she did not have all the hours yet that were required for night flying."

"Incredible," said Glen. "You know, even speaking to her casually around Ian's office, she is a very bright girl—but clearly a selfish girl as well. She certainly had the brains to orchestrate this whole mess."

"This makes sense. Robert being the murderer made no sense; he was too dumb. Let's go arrest her."

"It's too late to get a warrant," said Hans. "No judge is available to sign one."

"Let's get her in the morning then," said Glen. "Paige will go nowhere; she wants to collect her money and then she will bail out of town. She has no clue that we know what she did."

"Okay, boys. Let's get some sleep because tomorrow will be a big day."

Glen was en route home and received a call from Gail.

"What's going on? You promised me an exclusive on Ianova Industries, but it's been me investigating and getting my own stories. You asked me to stay away and I have. Come on. Throw me a bone. All I have is what all the other media has. Give me something."

"Okay," said Glen. "You are sounding like a whining child looking for milk or something."

"I am thirsty for something. What do you have for me?"

"Be at Ianova Industries tomorrow morning around ten. Wait in an unmarked car outside where no one recognizes you. Got it? No one must recognize you. When you see me and my boys walk in to Ianova Industries, follow us in and you will film a new arrest being made. You will be the first to have this story."

"Okay. Who is it that will be arrested?"

"Nice try, Gail. Good one."

"I will be there at ten tomorrow morning."

"Afterward, I will let you buy me lunch."

"I had no idea you were interested in a date with me," said Gail.

"Don't flatter yourself, girl. I want a free meal from you. Good-bye," said Glen.

Glen now is driving his car. A song comes on the radio. He starts remembering the names of the people who have died. He turns down the volume. *My Goodness, twenty-two murders.* Glen shook his head and a tear came rolling down his face. Glen shuts off the radio. *Ianova Industries should be shut down. It should be a place to go and remember those who were brutally murdered for money. This will go down as the biggest mass murder for personal gain in human history. I can't believe what has happened.*

Glen pulled into his driveway, got out of his car, and walked into his home. He threw down his keys, poured himself a strong one, and sat on the sofa. He turned on the TV and started channel surfing. All the news was about Ianova Industries. The media had given this a name: "Murder by Numbers."

"Yep," said Glen. "Murder by numbers was right—twenty-two to be exact and $275 million reasons." He shook his head.

That night, Glen was tossing and turning in bed. He couldn't get to sleep because too much was on his mind. He knew the warrant was coming in the morning and the pressure of a new arrest was huge.

* * *

Three detectives are talking in a coffee shop. They had to wait until 8:30 to see the judge.

"Well," said one officer. "It's 8:20. Let's go inside so we are first to see the judge so we can get our warrant."

The three officers went through the scanning process and showed their guns and badges to get through security. They made their way up to the judge's chambers and waited for him.

The judge had asked his receptionist to prepare all the paperwork that was required. He signed it and handed it over to the detectives. They headed to the police station and called Glen. Glen told them to bring the arrest warrant to Ianova Industries.

Glen was waiting for them in the parking lot. He got out of his car and made his way over to Gail's car. She was waiting for him.

Glen said, "Good morning, Gail. Are you ready?"

Gail said, "For our date?"

"No. It's too early! I told you yesterday not to flatter yourself."

"In that case, I am ready."

"This will go down in the history books as the most notorious murders for financial gain."

Glen walked into Ianova Industries with the cameraman behind him. He asked Vanity to get Paige over to the reception area.

Ian came out of his office and asked Glen what was going on.

Glen said, "You'll see in a second, Ian."

Paige walked into the office with lots of smiles and said good morning to everyone.

Glen said, "I can't believe you were the one, Paige."

"The one for what, Glen?"

"You are under arrest for the first-degree murder of twenty-two people named Tony Tuscony, Carrie Turner, Ellen Wolf, Blair Hinder—"

"Stop! I know all of them, Glen. I know who they are. Stop saying their names, it's bad enough they are all dead and then to hear you say their names? I can't swallow that."

Ian said, "What the heck, Paige? You think Paige did all this Glen?"

"Glen, one thing you are is mistaken, you are grossly mistaken."

"I was wrong with Robert, but I am not with Paige. The evidence against her is overwhelming."

"The evidence you have against me is a joke because I did nothing. You hear me?

Nothing. Am I being punked here? Is there a punch line? Are you guys joking?"

"Take her away."

The detectives placed Paige in handcuffs and proceeded outside. Gail and her cameraman followed them. They go through the front doors at Ianova Industries and what awaits them is an ocean of media. Cameras flashing, microphones crowding the faces of the detectives and of Paige. Gail wants to know how Paige masterfully orchestrated such overwhelming murders.

"Paige, how did you do it? How did you crash the plane in Arizona? I know you are a pilot."

Paige looked at Gail as if she saw a ghost.

"What the heck are you talking about? Both you and Glen have it all wrong. I did nothing. I killed no one. I am a pilot. You guys are hanging your hats on that? I know what a flap is, I know what a radio is, I know how hydraulics work so you classify me the murderer? The sad thing is Gail, while you and Glen think it is me that has murdered all these people, the real criminal, the real murderer is still out there mean while you are all here taking me in. Do I look like I can do what was done to the innocent victims?"

"You're guilty how can you deny this? The evidence against you spells Paige"

Paige looked around. She saw people who had been camping for days. They were protesting with signs in hopes of boycotting any sales that Ianova Industries may have. They were calling her a murderer. They wanted to kill her. She knew the crowd had already convicted her. She also knew that Glen Heron needed a arrest.

Glen opened the rear car door and helped Paige get in so she wouldn't bang her head. Paige shot a look at Gail.

Gail backed off and said, "Wow. That was weird. Did you feel the ice as well?"

The cameraman said, "Oh yeah. I did."

CHAPTER 17

Interrogation Time

At the police station, Glen wanted to be sure that things were done correctly and that all was in order. He wanted to be sure that Paige was not set free on a technicality.

He looked at Paige and said,

"There is the phone. Call whoever you need to call."

Paige said, "This is a joke and the real murderer is still out there."

"The murders will stop because you are in here and not out there killing people, Paige."

"Of course they will stop, you idiot. There is no one left to kill."

Glen pauses in an almost look of, wow, she is right, but remained firm in his conviction that Paige was the murderer, and the fact that she called him an idiot didn't help either.

"How do you know? How can you be sure with 3 of you still alive that the murders will stop?"

"It's a simple process of elimination. Glen, should I do your job? I'm alive. Mrs. Ianova and Robert Ianova are alive. There is no one else left in the lottery pool to kill."

"Yes there is, there is 3 of you left. You don't make any sense. Paige, it seems you can't answer why the murders will stop unless it is you that has done the killings. I am convinced that you are the murderer and I am convinced that because you are the murderer (Glen raises his voice now) that the killings will stop!"

Paige sat back into her chair and said, "I don't know why. I can't answer why the killings will stop. I know they will and I know I was not the one killing everyone"

"Is it because you are such an idiot that you can't answer the question—or is it because you are the murderer?"

"I want a lawyer,"

Glen slides the phone her way. In a very surprising move, Paige called Ianova Industries. Vanity answered the phone, and Paige asked for Ian.

Vanity said, "what is happening? Everyone here is in shock. What have you done, Paige? Is it true what they are saying about what you have done"

"I've done nothing wrong Vanity. Everyone here thinks I killed all those people. I wouldn't kill a fly for goodness sake—let alone my coworkers."

"Paige, Ian was told by Glen that there is evidence that you were involved in the plane crash and the other killings."

"Listen to me Vanity, Glen has taken so much heat for falsely arresting Robert and then having him released that he was starving to arrest someone because of the public outcry he was facing. The public wanted to see someone pay for those crimes. I firmly believe that I am the scapegoat for Glen's hideous investigation."

"How can you say it's hideous, Paige? Glen has been up for days with hardly any sleep trying to solve this thing."

"Of course it's hideous. It's obvious—isn't it? He has me in jail—doesn't he? Wait a minute. Do you think I did this stuff?"

"Well Paige, you said it. Afterall it is you in jail and no one else."

"Get me Ian Vanity."

"Just a moment I'll page him." *Murderer, does she think she can get away with this. That fake smile.*

Vanity pages Ian. "Yes Vanity what is it?:

"It is Paige Plane on the phone sir. She wants to speak with you sir" Rod Brown was also in Ian's office at this moment discussing things. "Wow," Ian said. He looks at Rod in shock. "What does she want, Vanity?"

"She wanted to speak to you, sir. I am not really sure what she wants"

Rod looked at Ian and said, "Take the call and put her on the speaker phone. Be sure to tell her that I am in your office with you in case this develops into something later. You can't hide that fact"

"That's why I pay you the big bucks. Good idea."

"Thanks, Vanity, put Paige's call through."

"Okay, sir."

"Hi, Paige. I want to tell you that you are on speaker phone. Rod Brown is with me in my office and will be listening to our conversation. Is that ok with you?"

"Oh, yes that is ok, that's great Ian. Hi, Rod."

"Hi, Paige, are they treating you well there?

"I guess they are treating me as well as can be expected. I wish I weren't here though. I wish I were back in my apartment waking up from a bad dream or something."

"Hey Paige you called for me. How can I help you"?

"As you saw this morning, I was arrested for all those murders. I didn't do it. I am innocent. I need a lawyer, and I am hoping that Rod can get me out of here the same way that Rod got Robert out of here."

"Do you mind if I answer that question, Ian?"

"Sure, I don't mind go ahead and answer it."

"It's more complicated than that, Paige. I am representing Robert. He is not out of the woods yet. He is out on bail, and I am 100 percent sure that the charges will all be dropped, but formally that has not happened yet because the paperwork is not always as fast as we would like it to be. However, I cannot represent you because it would be a conflict of interest. I can't represent you and Robert."

"I understand that Rod. So get me someone else in your office that can."

"Sorry, I will not do that. I own my firm Paige. When my firm stands behind someone, it is actually me standing behind my firm. The conflict will still exist"

Paige pauses in disbelief.

"Ian, can you refer me to someone else please since Rod can't help me?"

Ian looks at Rod for an answer. Rod says nothing but gestures and mouths the word, no!

"Paige, I—and Ianova Industries—need to distance ourselves from this situation."

"What situation, Ian? I am innocent—damn it. I need your help. I have been working for you for over fifteen years. I have not asked you for anything., I need your help now. Help me, Ian. Please, help me"

Ian looked around the room and said, "I can't help you with this one, Paige."

Paige is shocked. It's as if the room is spinning around her. She hung up the phone.

Glen looked at her and said,

"Ian won't help you? All those years of service and he is hanging you out to dry?"

"Well Glen, I guess you have what you need. I guess you have your girl."

"I know I do. It just feels nice to see you squirm"

"Call Gail boys. Let's set up a news conference," said Glen.

Glen was surrounded by detectives and others at reception area at headquarters. One of the officers said, "Wow. I would never have guessed that Paige was the killer. In fact, she would be the last person that I would suspect was the killer."

"It is always the people you last suspect that will surprise you the most with their actions. Okay, let's get lunch, people. Good work. Set the conference for four o'clock. Let's order pizza. I am starved."

They break apart now and some go to their offices and some go wash up in the bathroom. Glen looks at Hans as they are the only two left in the room, "I wonder who Paige will get to represent her. What do you think Hans? Have you seen her on the phone trying to reach someone else after she spoke to Ian?"

"She has been on the phone quite a bit. I understand that a lawyer was en route here and will actually make the news conference. Actually it doesn't matter who she got; the evidence is too large. She killed all of them!"

"She sure did."

* * *

They all went and ate pizza in the cafeteria lunch room area. One of the girls in the room asks Glen, how many years he thinks that Paige will get in prison? Hans walks into the room and whispers something into Glen's ear.

"I can't hear you from all this noise Hans, speak a little louder"

"Paige's lawyer is here and in the meeting room talking with her." Glen ignores Hans but just nods his head to acknowledge what he said. Glen responds while still chewing his pizza to the girl who asked about the prison sentence.

"Fifteen years per person x 22 people is how many years Hans?"

Hans gets a calculator out and punches in the figures and responds "330 years." Glen still chewing his pizza says, "She could get 330 years, but she will get out on good behaviour in say, 150 years. But really at the end of the day, she will probably get all twenty-two life sentences. She will never see outside again if I have anything to do with it." A bunch of wow, and incredible murmurs permeates throughout the kitchenette area.

"Let's get out of here and get ready for this conference. It's almost time."

Glen made his way into the bathroom, washed his hands, and started to fix his hair. *I am so happy that this is finally over.*

Three detectives walked out to the seating area. Glen stood at the podium. There is a massive media frenzy.

Glen starts the press conference.

"There have been twenty-two murders committed. All twenty-two dead people were employees of Ianova Industries. All twenty-two were winning lottery ticket holders of a $275 million grand prize. The total number of participants in the pool was 25. The lottery split was to be $ 11 million dollars to each winner. We initially arrested Robert Ianova. Evidence suggested that Robert was not the mastermind behind all these killings. Through intensive investigative work, and with new evidence that had been brought forward, we arrested Ms. Paige Plane for the murders of all twenty-two people. We have proof that places Paige at scenes where the murders have been either orchestrated or took place. Don't let Paige's good looks, warm smile, or charming personality fool you into thinking that she is a warm, fuzzy, and friendly individual. She is a cold, calculated murderer. We have evidence that will prove that. We will show that Ms. Paige Plane had acess to the airport, that she had knowledge how to sabatoge and bring a plane down from the sky causing the loss of life to all on board. I am sure that you all have many questions. We are still piecing puzzles together. I cannot comment on the specifics until the pieces are altogether. Go ahead and ask away and I hope that I can answer your questions."

"Did anyone else have the same access as Paige to the same part of the airport? And, what if someone was flying on a private jet or taking flying lessons? Didn't they have the same access as Ms. Plane did Detective?"

"It is possible, but Paige had the knowledge of how to sabotage the plane."

"Isn't it true that you didn't even investigate all persons who entered the airport that could be potential suspects?"

"We are narrowing that part of our investigation down"

"Could it be that this part of your investigation is the part of the many pieces of the puzzle you are still trying to piece together because you really have no clue or evidence that it was Paige who sabotaged the plane? Also, pieces of the puzzle are still missing and broken for the Bixby accident and the plant accidents—aren't they detective?"

"Who are you sir?"

"I am Ed Anderson, Paige's lawyer."

The crowd was humming and hawing. They all look to Glen for a response.

"There are pieces to put together; however, all the pieces are there. Paige even told me to my face that I had my girl—referring to herself—in front of these three detectives."

"He said she said. Besides, didn't she say that to you after Rod Brown and Ian denied helping her with her unfounded arrest? Didn't she mean it facetiously because she was shocked to be arrested in the first place because she was innocent? Don't you think she felt that the whole world was caving in on her with no one to turn to for help? I guess you have your girl, Glen?"

"No more questions," said Glen. He walked away, and his detectives followed him.

Ed Anderson turned to face the crowd and said, "Make no mistake, people. Paige Plane is innocent. The police have only circumstantial evidence that I will squash. She will be free soon."

Glen was going way too fast without proper investigative work to arrest another innocent person. He made a big mistake arresting Robert Ianova and he just made a bigger mistake arresting Ms. Paige Plane."

CHAPTER 18

Interrogating Paige

Glen was so upset that he went into his office and slammed the door. He looked up at the ceiling and yelled.

Glen paged Hans and said, "Get Paige and her lawyer into the interrogating room. I have some questions for her."

"Okay. Give me ten minutes and then come on in," said Hans.

Glen shuffled through some paperwork in his office and whispered, "I have no time for this crap." He dropped the paperwork onto his desk, made his way into the kitchenette, and took a bite of cold pizza. "That sucks cold. He poured himself a cup of coffee and took a sip. "That tastes like old socks."

Hans said, "I didn't know you knew what old socks tastes like, Glen."

"Ha! Not funny buddy"

Hans said, "The interrogating room is ready. Paige and Ed are in there."

As they entered the interrogating room, Ed said, "Why don't you just release Paige now, and I will promise not to embarrass the both of you and this police organization?"

Glen said, "Don't you want justice to be served, Ed?"

Ed said, "Of course I want justice to be served. There are twenty-two people dead out there, for Goodness sakes Glen. What kind of a stupid question is that?"

"Then help me serve that justice, Ed," we investigated these crimes; all evidence points to Ms. Plane. I can't help it if we were wrong with that evidence. You seem to think we are wrong. You will have to tell me where we are wrong so we can serve justice together. All I want is the right person to pay for these crimes. Right now unless you show me otherwise, it is Paige. Can I ask Paige some questions now, Ed?"

"Of course. Go ahead."

"Paige, the night before the plane crash, did you go to the airport?"

"No."

"We saw your name on the security sheets. That indicates that you were there. What is it? The security sheets were wrong—or are you lying to me right now?"

"I was there during the day—you asked if I was there at night. I was not there at night."

Glen made some notes. "Did you go to the mechanic's area?"

"Yes," answered Paige.

"Why did you go there?"

"I wanted to say hi to Leo Chuckhill."

"You mean the airline mechanic who signed off on the plane that crashed as airworthy?

That same Leo Chuckhill?"

"Don't lead her on Glen" interjects Ed! "It's ok Ed I have nothing to hide" replies Paige.

"Yes, that is the same Leo Glen."

"Now that is very interesting to me Paige." Glen makes more notes.

"Why did you want to say hi to Leo?"

"Because I like Leo. Ever since I have been taking flying lessons, I grew a liking to Leo.

He always comes over to say hi whenever he sees me. He signs off on my plane. Since I take lessons, we have aircraft in common and I wanted to meet this guy and get to know him a bit better. I think he likes me to. We might actually date."

"Not while in here you won't, Paige."

Ed interjects, "Watch the innuendos, Glen."

"Do you know about the hydraulics of a plane, Paige?"

"I do."

"Are you aware of drain positioning on a hydraulic switch?"

"I am."

"How do you know about that?"

"Leo told me. He filled me in about the plane crash and why it crashed. He showed me a similar switch on another aircraft and how it works."

"You mean that at the time of the crash, you had no idea how this switch operated?"

"Well, I had an idea I suppose. I know it exists, I know it is there, but how does it operate? I guess I know the purpose it serves but hey, don't ask me to explain it's mechanical functionality."

"When did Leo show you this mechanism?"

"Right after you went to see him. I had flying lessons that same afternoon."

"Yes, but you work and can't fly at night. How could you go for lessons that afternoon when dark was fast approaching?"

"I can fly at night with an instructor beside me. However, the lesson was in the afternoon.

Night was not an issue. My lesson was from 4pm to 5pm"

"I think you are lying, Paige," "Liar" Yelled out Hans.

"Control your man Glen," said Ed. "I won't take this. Paige is talking to you out of generosity. I will answer on her behalf next time with one word answers if you would like."

"No, it's okay," said Glen. "Right, Hans?"

"Yes, sir," said Hans.

Paige continues, "On that day Leo showed me how the switch operated and he showed me what went wrong with the plane, and why it crashed. I was very shaken about that. I gained knowledge at that time as to how the switch actually operates."

Glen said, "Everyone was shaken. There were a lot of lives lost for the wrong reasons.

Paige, do you know how to change saw blades or how scaffolding works at Ianova Industries?"

"I do."

"How do you know?"

"I have been working there for over fifteen years. I did inventory once a year. I watched employees strengthen and replace scaffolding. I watched them change saw blades as well."

"Why would you watch a saw blade being changed? How would that be useful to you?"

"I found it interesting. I don't know why."

"Why don't you ask her about the Bixby Killings Glen?"

"Still piecing that one together, Ed. Paige, by the way, have you ever driven a Cadillac Escalade or a Ford F-150?"

"No—neither vehicle,"

Glen looked disheartened. He needed to place Paige in both vehicles or at least prove that she had orchestrated the involvement of the two vehicles. "Why didn't you go on the trip to Arizona?"

"I wanted to save my vacation time for the end of the year."

"But you would receive millions of dollars through the lottery. Why would saving vacation time be a concern?"

"Money was not the concern. I did not want to desert the work order department. Most people were going on that trip. I couldn't do that to Mr. Ianova. Leave the department alone? No, I couldn't."

"Paige, you answered these questions quite well, but I cannot get my head around one big issue."

"What is it Glen, ask me"

"You called Rita Wilson of The Lottery Corporation at 10:30 am regarding the explosion at Rex's house, that is a full thirteen minutes before the explosion ever happened. You told her to take Rex Hill's name off of the list of winners. You told Vanity that Rex's home exploded because of a gas leak. The investigation wasn't even completed then.

How did you know his home blew up? How did you know there was a gas leak?"

Hans and Ed turn in unison towards Paige. Especially Ed, he seems very anxious to hear Paige's reply, but catches himself now and he yelled, "Stop! I want to discuss this with my client first. Don't answer those two last questions. You don't have to."

"Come on, Ed," yelled Glen. "You said you wanted justice to be served here, damn it. Let her answer the questions and maybe we can all go home from here."

"It's okay," said Paige. "That's very easy to answer. It's okay. Let me answer it."

"Okay. Go ahead," said Ed.

"Adam Wendell told me about Rex's home blowing up and that it was gas that caused the explosion."

Everyone zeroed in on Glen. The whole room was spinning around him.

"Who exactly is Adam Wendell?"

"He is the president of Stain Refinishers," replied Paige.

Everyone took a deep breath; they couldn't believe there was another potential suspect out there that hadn't been questioned.

Glen said, "I remember him now. He hangs with Ian a bit. I have seen him around Ian's office periodically. How did it come about that Adam told you these things?"

"A bunch of suppliers came into the office unannounced that morning demanding a meeting with Mr. Ianova because of all the money he owed them. I heard rumors that they would threaten a class action lawsuit against Mr. Ianova. Adam came over and asked me how my flying lessons were going. I told him they were going okay. He asked me if I had heard about Rex Hill. I asked Adam what he meant by that, and he said that his home blew up because of a gas leak. I was very upset about that. Vanity paged the suppliers to go into Ian's office, and I called Rita. The call had to be made—and it was me looking after the list. I was delegated to call Rita. I don't think that this was a crime."

Glen said, "Did Ianova Industries owe Adam a lot of money?"

"I don't know what he was owed, but I know that stain and lacquers were the most expensive components to finishing millwork. Ian was always talking to the plant guys to try to watch out for waste on stains. I know it must hurt us when too much of the finishes were used."

"How well do you know Adam, Paige?"

"Well Glen I guess you can say I know him quite well., A few times he took me on a flight on his plane and let me take over the wheel. It was such a high for me to do that, so eventually I started to take flying lessons. I love it to. So I guess you can say that it is because of Adam introducing me to planes is what started my love of flying. I can't wait to get into the air again."

"Do you and Adam have feelings for each other?"

"It's not like that, Glen. Adam was too old for me. Ever since his wife died, he was looking for companionship—nothing more. He made absolutely no advances toward me. He was a true gentleman looking to help out—that's all."

"How old would you say Adam is?"

"About your age, Glen."

Glen looked at Hans and Ed, and they all smiled.

Glen said, "Wait, Paige. I am not old."

Paige laughed. She said, "I am thirty-five. I guess I consider anyone who has a few years on me an old person."

Everyone in the room smiled at that response.

"How do you know his wife died?"

"There was a funeral two years ago. Most of the staff at Ianova Industries went to it. It was really sad."

"How old was she when she died?"

"I think around forty or so."

"That was young," said Glen. "How did she die?"

"It was cancer. Adam had no kids, so he devoted his time to growing his company. He spent a lot of his time there, and some say that he even sleeps there sometimes. His only peace comes when he flies, so other than his company, his other babies are his planes. He has several planes; I think about three or four planes. One of them is a jet. He never let me take the wheel of that one."

I guess not," said Glen. "It must be pretty expensive to own a jet."

Paige said, "I'm sure Adam has lots of coin because he flies to his place in Italy, Virgin Islands, Greece, Panama, Bahamas, and some other places for weekends."

"He owns homes in all the places you mentioned?"

"Yep, he does," said Paige. "I have not been to them, but he told me about them."

"Wow. What did I do wrong in life? One guy has so much, and others can't find a meal. Incredible, life isn't fair sometimes. Incidentally Paige, what kind of vehicle does Adam drive?"

"A big BMW is his everyday car, but he bought a Cadillac Escalade for when he needs to bring stuff home."

"Do you know the color, Paige?"

"It is gorgeous bright pearl white."

Han's eyes and Glen's eyes almost popped out of their heads. They looked at each other with stunned looks.

Glen said, "Call the judge. Get an arrest warrant for Adam Wendell. Oh my goodness. I can't believe this. This guy's baby, his company, has been hit hard by Ian not paying him. He was killing all these people in hopes of Ian getting all the money so he could afford to pay his suppliers. What a master plan, damn it. Go arrest him, boys."

"Can we get out of here? Is Paige free to go?"

"Yeah. Go on. Get out of here. Hans, let's go get Adam."

CHAPTER 19

The Search for Adam

Adam Wendell was sitting in a chair in Ian's office. Adam closed up his laptop and slid it into a laptop carrying case. He stood up and reached across Ian's desk to shake hands with Ian.

Ian said, "Adam, I am very excited that we worked this out between us. You have been a friend to me for many years. I am truly sorry how we treated you by not paying you and the troubles I caused you. I hope what I did just now proves that I truly value our friendship."

"Yes. I am also very happy that we worked this out. I was very worried that you would leave me out there hanging to shut my company down. You know my company is my baby."

"Yes I know it is as my company is my baby to"

"Well Ian thank you very much for looking after me like you said you would. Now I must go back to my office to sign a few checks since I have some money now."

"OK Adam, take care and we'll see you soon my friend"

"Cheers"

Adam made his way into his car and started driving away from Ianova Industries.

* * *

Glen left the police station with Hans and called dispatch for the address of Adam Wendell's home. Glen put the hammer down and started driving very fast with the siren blaring en route to Adam's house.

"We can finally end this thing and put these murders behind us."

"I hope we have the right person this time Glen"

"Is there any doubt that Adam is the killer Hans? You heard Paige, what doubt do you still have?"

Glen was driving so fast that he was going sideways around corners. Hans was holding on for dear life but said nothing about the driving because he knew that Glen needed this guy behind bars.

Hans said, "Glen, I bet Ed, Paige's lawyer already called the media to say that we are going to arrest Adam."

"No. I told him to give me two hours to keep his trap shut. He promised that he would."

"You think he is a man of his word, Glen?"

"He had better be. If he isn't, I will arrest him for obstruction of justice."

"Fair enough. That sounds pretty solid to me."

Glen pulled into Adam's driveway. He had shut off his siren before getting onto Adam's street so as to not draw attention. They made their way to the front door and rang the bell.

"You think this is a good idea Glen? We don't have the warrant yet."

"Don't worry Hans, you worry too much. I received a text, it's signed."

* * *

Adam pulled into the parking lot at Stain Refinishers. He went inside to speak to Brian Cutter. "Adam, we are done here. Here is your check."

Adam said, "If it is all the same to you, Brian, please keep your check and let's wire the money straight into my account. I have my laptop here with me so it will be easy to do."

"Ok sure why not Adam. Let me call Theresa, she is a wiz at this stuff."

"Sure."

Theresa was called and comes into the office.

Brian said, "Wire the money into Adam's account. Can you do that?"

"Sure I can. Adam that is your laptop?

"Yes it is Theresa"

"Go ahead and log into your account, and I will get your transit and account number. Do you have the swift transfer number with you?"

"Sure I do it's right here. There you go."

Theresa went and got her laptop and said, "Give me two seconds to log into our account and I will start the wiring process."

* * *

At Adam's house, Glen and Hans realized that no one was home. Glen looked into the garage from a small window and said, "Holy crap. Look at this Glen. That's the Cadillac Escalade—and it's the right color."

"I didn't even know that Adam bought one of these things. I thought he drove that Jaguar or Beemer or whatever they are called.

Let's go see Ian. I bet he knows exactly where Adam is. I am sure that Adam is in constant communication with Ian because Ian owes him a ton of money."

"Why not call him? Why do we need to drive there?"

"If Adam is there, I don't want to give him a heads up that we are coming."

"I guess you're right Glen,".

"OK, let's go then."

Glen and Hans get into their vehicle and start to make their way towards Ianova Industries.

* * *

"Okay, Adam. The money is in there. Check to see"

"Thank you Theresa, let me just quickly do that. The balance is yes, it's in there."

"Are you satisfied that the entire deposit is in your account?"

"Yes Brian, it looks like $85 million is in there, thank you very much"

Theresa said, "Adam, what are you hiding from? That's a big deposit into a Swiss account that you don't want anyone to know about."

For a few seconds, Adam looked right into Theresa's eyes as if he could kill her for asking that question. Brian noticed the chill and looked like he was about to say something.

Adam put on a smile and said, "Are you kidding me? You paid off my three-year loan on my little black-and-white television."

Everyone burst out into laughter. Brian shook Adam's hand and so did Theresa.

"What are you going to do with all that money?" asked Brian.

"I am on my way to the airport. I will go to my Bahamas home for a week and think about it."

"Take your time—and have a great trip."

Adam drove off in his Beemer out of his old company that he just sold off, Stain Refinishers.

As Glen and Hans were driving toward Ianova Industries, a car headed toward them., It was Adam; but Glen noticed the car and at the same time paid no real attention to it. The car passes and Glen also looks into his rear view mirror and sees the car again but did not associate that it was Adam. Glen pulls into Ianova Industries and rushes in to see Ian with Hans and just passes right by Vanity and straight into Ian's office.

"Do you know where Adam is? Adam is the murderer—I need him now. Where is he?"

"I just wired him $25 million and you are standing here telling me that he is the murderer?"

"What do you mean you wired him twenty-five large?".

"I owed him about $20 million, so I agreed to give him another $5 million for futures because I had caused big financial turmoil at his company. Since I am getting a bunch of money from the lottery through my son and my wife, I paid him out of my personal account for now."

"Wow," said Glen. "His plan worked perfectly."

"What do you mean?" asked Ian.

"He killed everyone in the lottery pool except your family members because he knew your family would bail you out."

"How would he even know who was on the lottery pool list?" asked Ian.

"Easy,. he was friends with Paige. She told him."

"Wow," said Ian. "I did find it kind of odd that we wired the money into a Swiss account."

"Can you trace it back or somehow get it back?"

"No, it can't be done. That's why people use those types of accounts. To difficult to trace. It can take weeks even with federal assistance."

"Where is he now or where is he headed. Do you know?"

"Yes. He was going to his office to sign a few checks because he has the money now. He left here about twenty minutes ago. You can catch him at his office."

"Where is his office?" asked Hans.

"Two miles from here. Go left out of my driveway and drive for exactly 2 miles and you will see Stain Refinishers on your right. I clocked it, 2 miles bang on."

Glen and Hans run out of Ianova Industries and get into their car and start driving toward Adam's office. They burned rubber as they leave left.

When Adam pulled into security at the airport, he showed his ID. He received clearance and went to his hangar.

"Good afternoon, Mr. Wendell," said a groundskeeper. "Your plane is ready at the secured runway as you asked. I will take you over."

"Lets go" says Adam.

As they drive away from the hanger on a golf cart they travel a few minutes, they go through another secured semi screening area. The scanner scans them and now a gate opens automatically and they drive through.

"Mr. Wendell, as you know that's as far as I can take you sir. You have your security card with you, sir? You need it to open the next gate."

"Yes I do," answered Adam.

"Bye, sir. Have a great flight. I believe you are cleared for takeoff in fifteen minutes, sir."

"Thanks. I have to go through preflight schedules. The timing couldn't be more perfect."

Glen pulled into Stain Refinishers and ran into the office.

"Where is Adam Wendell?" he yelled.

Brian came out of his office and said, "Who the hell are you yelling like that?"

"I am Detective Glen Herron, and I need Adam Wendell. He is wanted for murdering twenty-two people. Do you know where he is?"

"Oh my goodness. I just wired him $85 million."

"Why?" said Glen. "Who are you?"

"I am Brian Cutter. I have been after Adam to buy this company for a couple years. It was worth over $150 million, but I paid $85 million. It was a great deal so I took it."

"How about the creditors?"

"I settled for twenty cents on the dollar."

"How much you think Adam made by not paying them?"

"Probably $40 million."

"Wow—that's 150 large when you consider what he got from Ian. When did you wire the money?"

"I wired him the money twenty minutes ago. He was here with his laptop. Here is the check. He wanted the money wired instead."

"Let me guess—into a Swiss account?"

"That's right," said Brian.

"Do you know where he is?"

"He told me he was going to fly to his place in the Bahamas for a week to think about what to do with the money."

Glen looked at Hans and said, "Let's go to the airport."

They burned rubber toward the airport.

"Can you believe this, Hans?"

"I have never seen such a masterful plan. Adam Wendell is a very smart man."

"He is a cold, calculated murderer—a selfish man. Sure, he was smart—he ran a successful company and made millions off of it."

"My fear is that this guy is so smart that he will be gone without a trace by the time we get to the airport."

"Have no fear, Hans. One thing you can never do is escape the clutches of the law. One way or another, the law will always come up and bite you in the ass—regardless of where you are and what you are trying to hide. Remember Enron? Those criminals are all behind bars. They thought that they could get away with all their criminal activity, get rich, and rip off the average person. Look at where they are. They are in the same place that Adam will be when we cuff him at the airport. You know what else, Hans? I may accidentally bang his head on our car roof and break some of his teeth. There might be an unusually long booking time before he receives medical help. Maybe we will all get lucky and he'll bleed to death instead of wasting the taxpayers' money by keeping him alive in prison. This is where Texas had it right; the death penalty would have made Adam think twice about what he was doing."

"I don't know about that, Glen. Look at Robert Ianova. Imagine if he was wrongfully convicted by the evidence we had? The wrong guy would have been executed. What if Paige was convicted on the evidence that we had—and it was compelling evidence. She would have been executed as well. Both of them—wrongfully executed. That's why perhaps Texas had it wrong!"

You mentioned Enron. Think for a moment of the tens of thousands of people who were scammed out of their life savings. People who may have committed suicide because of losing their life savings, those who have had their retirement life style change, those who can't tune up their car or can't give it a oil change or can't buy a new one even though they easily could have prior to Enron, those who now scrimp" Yes I get it Hans"

"You think those bigwigs at Enron deserved the death penalty Glen? They superficially killed a lot of people."

"I don't know Hans but I will tell you this, you sure got alot stored upstairs there"

"Well I guess Life isn't as fair as we honest people would like it to be. I guess we have our own ideas about how we think we can make it better. All we can do is our best."

CHAPTER 20

The Airport

Glen and Hans pulled into the airport. They drove to the area where the aircraft owners parked their jets and took flying lessons. They were in line to go through the security gate, but four cars were in front of them. Glen started honking his horn. This actually made things go slower; the security guard left his post and looked to see who the horn honker was.

The guard yelled, "Slow it down, buddy, or you will never get through. Be patient."

Glen showed his badge to the guard, but the guard didn't pay much attention to it.

Their turn, finally comes up to speak to the guard and Glen unleashes and starts yelling that they are there to apprehend a criminal and if the criminal gets away that Glen will arrest him with obstruction. Glen now asked, "Have you seen Adam Wendell come through here?"

"Yes, I have sir, he went to his hangar."

"Point me in the direction of his hanger"

"It is that way detective, it is hanger number two."

The guard flipped open the security gate and Glen drove as fast as he could toward the hangar.

They arrive at the hanger and both Glen and Hans get out of the car. The first person they saw was Leo Chuckhill. The same plane mechanic who signed off on the doomed Arizona flight. Leo sees them walking towards him and says,

"To what do I owe the pleasure of seeing you two here? You come to put cuffs on and arrest me?"

"Not quite," said Glen. "Do you know where Adam Wendell is?"

"I do," said Leo. "I signed off on his plane." He showed Glen a clipboard of all the things he had checked off on the jet.

"Is it normal to have all these safety things performed?"

"It sure is," replied Leo. "I spend my days checking my own work against procedures and checking my guys' work against procedure lists. Remember, you can't pull over in the sky and try to fix a problem if one occurs. I need to be sure that the plane is airworthy when it leaves my hangar. Otherwise I wouldn't need you to arrest me, sir. I would be blood guilty on my own personal trial."

"I hear you," said Glen. "I see you really care about this stuff. Sorry for being so insensitive earlier to you. Do you know where Adam was preparing his plane for?"

"He told me that he was going to his place in the Bahamas for a week."

"Where is he?" asked Glen.

"He booked a private runway for himself."

"Point me in the direction."

"Pointing won't help, Glen. Your car won't take you to the area you need to be. It is too wide to fit. We need to take you there in a golf cart. That's how you get there."

"Get me a golf cart then. Come on. Let's go."

Leo got his pager and said, "Golf cart to hangar two. Golf cart to hangar two please. I have two police detectives waiting."

Someone at the other end replies, "coming, I will be there in less than a minute." "Roger on that" replies Leo. Glen asked, "Where is the ride coming from?"

"From the hangar next door. That's where the rides come from that service all eight hangars."

"Why do we need a golf cart to take us to where Adam is?" asked Glen.

Leo said, "It is a secured runway for VIP's. No cars allowed—in fact, you will need to go through additional screening once you get there."

* * *

Adam walked into the cockpit and said to the pilot sitting in the seat, "There has been a change of plans. I will take it from here. I will be taking this trip solo. You can go."

"But the Bahamas private airport is tricky, sir. You need to bring it in low over the mountains and drop it fast to the runway. I am experienced with that."

"I know," said Adam. "I've landed there hundreds of times. I am pretty sure I can handle it."

"Okay, sir. You are the boss. Everything is ready. The engine pressure is perfect. I went through all the safety procedures. The control tower is waiting on my word that you are on board. We already have runway clearance. I guess this it. Have a great flight, sir."

"Thank you," said Adam as the pilot turned and began his walk out of the plane. Now Adam shifted his eyes toward all the gauges of the plane and visually sees that they seem to be in order and begins to flip a few switches but has not yet sat down.

Glen and Hans began their short ride to Adam's plane. They got to the additional screening area. The gate in front of the cart would not open.

Glen said, "What is wrong here? Why won't the gate open?"

The driver said, "You must have guns on you. The gate won't open because of it. Leave your guns here on the table and pick them up on your way back."

"We won't leave our guns here," said Glen. Trip the switch!"

"It's computerized sir. There are no humans here. I can't trip the switch. You have got to leave your guns here—then the gate will open automatically."

"You mean to tell me that no one can carry guns through here—even the rich wealthy people coming through with their personal security guards?"

The driver said, "Oh no, sir. Many people come through with guns, but they have presecurity clearances and a card that will open the gate."

"Great," said Glen. "Leave your gun here, Hans." Glen pulled his gun out of his holster. They left them in the box.

"How do we get the guns back?"

"You get them from security once exiting. This box when closed automatically goes down below ground to a conveyor belt right back to security. It's easy."

Glen was visibly upset about the whole thing, but he realized that this kind of tight security was required for a smooth operation.

The driver said, "There is Mr. Wendell's airplane. It sure is a beauty. Sure would be nice to have Mr. Wendell's money."

"Where Mr. Wendell is going, his money will be of no use to him."

"Why, where is he going?"

"I can't say as yet. However it will all become public knowledge real soon." Glen just looks forward as he sees Adam's plane in front of him. Glen says, "I got you now, you coward."

They approached a gate that separated them from the runway.

"Okay. Give me your gate entry card, and I will put it in the slot."

Glen said, "I have no card."

The driver said, "You can't go past here without one."

"You don't have a card?" asked Glen.

"No, sir. You have to get one from the security office."

Glen looked at the fence and said, "Great. We can't climb it either. Look at the size of the barbed wire at the top."

"No, sir. You can't climb that."

Glen walked toward the thick metal gate. He shook it violently, but it barely moved.

Adam stuck his head out of the plane to pull up the stairs for takeoff. He sees Glen staring at him. Both make eye contact and it is chilling. Glen wants Adam real bad. Adam says,

"Detective Glen Heron, are you here to investigate something?"

"You are under arrest, Adam Wendell, for the first-degree murders of twenty-two innocent lives at Ianova Industries."

"Yeah, yeah, yeah. Tell me something I don't know. Come arrest me then. What are you waiting for? Oh wait, detective, you didn't get preauthorized clearance—did you? You can't come get me?" You think I'm an idiot to leave a loose end like something simple as security clearance? Na, I'm much to bright to make it that easy for you Glen"

"No Adam, I don't think you are an idiot. In fact I think the opposite. You are brilliant, Adam! Hiding behind a fence. Killing all those people—all those innocent people—so Ian could get the big prize from his son and his wife to pay all his debts, including yours. Excellent foresight you had on that one, Adam. You truly are a very smart man"

"Thank you for the compliment, Glen. Think about it. It was a no-brainer. What family wouldn't help another family member with all that money? That was the easy part of my plan. Getting rid of 22 others, well that took some planning. I stayed up a few hours past my bed time to come up with a plan for them"

"Then you had another brilliant move Adam, selling off all your company's assets. Wow—you walked away with over a hundred million dollars. And in another brilliant move, you deposited it all into Swiss bank accounts so we couldn't trace anything. Well we could actually trace your accounts, in a year maybe. But by then you would have created such a world web that we would never solve how and where you moved money. Have I missed anything?"

"You did, actually Glen. I want to thank you again for all those compliments. It is not too often you get recognized for brilliance from your local police department."

"Enough," said Glen. "I am being facetious, you murderer."

"No need for name calling," said Adam. "Let me answer your question before you rudely interrupt me again. I don't like being interrupted. Show some respect for my brilliance. You did leave something out—your totals were way off. After raiding my own bank accounts, coming up with some fake loans and empty exaggerated lines of credit, and selling some of my most expensive real estate,

I have well over five hundred million dollars—not one hundred. I even sold my house and through in the Escalade. I think I can make a pretty good life for myself somewhere. Don't you think, Glen?"

"You are a brilliant man, Adam. Why not work your way out of your financial woes? Why kill all those innocent people?"

"My wife died very early in life. I had no kids; my new marriage was to my company. Sure, I had a call girl here and there or a girlfriend here and there—but nothing I wanted to keep, except my company. She was good to me; we became very successful. I didn't need money; it was all a game for me. I had all the money I ever needed. I had homes all over the world. I dove into my work and made a success of it. I made a fortune—more money than I knew what to do with."

"So why kill all those innocent people?"

"In life, one thing you can never do is control the actions of other people. You can control your own destiny, but I couldn't control the poor business decisions of Ian Ianova. Ian was a great guy, but Ian was a very stupid businessman. He was no match for the smarts of his old man. No comparison there. He started to cost me a lot of money. He started to rip me off by not paying me. I started to do the same with my suppliers. Ian ruined my company. It's amazing. You can do so many things right, but when someone else does so many things wrong, it affects you. And it affected me personally. I wasn't going to put up with it any longer."

"You are not going to the Bahamas—are you?"

Adam looked at Glen and started to pull up the stairs of his aircraft. "All the paperwork says I am going to the Bahamas."

The door shut, and Adam walked toward the cockpit and sat down in the pilot's chair. Glen called headquarters and said, "Make sure the plane can't leave—or track it."

Adam slid open a window and smiled.

Glen hung up his cell and said, "You realize you need to land somewhere. You will be tracked on radar or satellite somewhere. I will find you—and you will pay for what you have done."

"I don't think so. After I am in the air, this radio will be shut off. My beacons are already shut down. My radar is off. I will be flying in stealth mode with maps and charts only. No one can trace me. I am brilliant don't forget, you said so yourself twice."

"You are a murderer and a warning, always have eyes in the back of your head. Whatever you do, wherever you eat, wherever you sleep, wherever you drive, shave, or swim, one day, I will be there to cuff you."

"Ha!" replies Adam with a smile. Now Adam's face turns devilish and replies, "I don't think so, Glen., where I am going and what is waiting for me at the other end, I will die of old age in a fun-filled life. Remember one thing, detective Glen Heron" Adam proceeds to close his window slowly as the jet engines rev up slightly. "Those people who say that crime does not pay, they are wrong. Dead wrong!"

Adam closed the window; the jet engines rev up and Adam's airplane blasts down the runway toward the sun and becomes airborne. Glen and Hans stared at the plane as it climbed towards altitude.

Glen looked at Hans and said, "We'll get him eventually."

THE END